HEARTBREAK KINGS

SEDONA VENEZ

WANT FREE SEDONA VENEZ BOOKS?

Sign up for Sedona Venez's Newsletter and receive FREE BOOKS. In addition to the free stories, you will also get special pricing, exclusive previews and news of new releases.

GET A FREE SEDONA VENEZ BOOK!

Join Sedona's mailing list to be the first to know of new releases, free books, special prices and other author giveaways.

https://sedonavenez.com/free-book

CHAPTER 1

SABINE

A THRONG of irate college boys congregated outside the dormitory as Mom drove our battered truck past on the way to the parking lot. There were fewer of them than I had expected, maybe a dozen huffy, scowling faces, half a dozen signs, and a bunch of yelling. Mom's eyes widened as she watched them.

"Wow, those boys are crazy! Maybe this isn't such a good idea. You say the word, and I'll bring you back home." Her delicate features strained with worry as she watched some boys turn to glare at our car. One of them threw something that bounced off the truck bed—maybe a rock, maybe something else.

"Mama, I can't. You know that." There was too much riding on my coming to this place. Markinswell University, a not-quite Ivy League school on Long Island. I enrolled here with the only full-ride scholarship I had been offered. My only chance for college now that Dad died and Mom was struggling upstate. They included everything—books, housing, transportation allowance, even a small amount of discretionary funds. There was just one little catch...

"Those boys don't want you here, Sabine. You're the only woman on campus except for some staff. You know how boys are in groups. You'll be the only girl." I could hear the fear in her voice, and I knew where it came from.

"Mama, please. This isn't Hell's Kitchen or Port-au-Prince. There's a lot more security—" I started, but she cut me off.

"It doesn't have to be as bad as either to still be bad. Even with the security men and the cameras, young men are young men. They're nice to look at, but they're not nice." She waved a hand dismissively as she rounded the corner toward the parking lot.

"I can handle myself," I insisted gently, pleadingly, hiding my simmering annoyance that she thought I couldn't.

She nodded slowly, frowning as she drove. "You're a smart girl, Sabine, and tough, but there are so many of them. You know what men will do when they are angry, and there are a lot of them. You have seen." Her voice trembled just a little with emotion.

I leaned back in my seat and closed my eyes. "Yeah, Mama. I know." I did. Hell's Kitchen, back when Dad was alive, when I was ten. Rioting in the streets after the Cartwright assassination. How Mom and Dad had piled furniture against the door and stuck me in the bathtub with a mattress on top of me. Hearing the gunshots, the glass breaking, the men outside screaming. Smelling the smoke.

Mama had a lot of reasons to fear a repeat performance. The Cartwright riots had been only one example of the things she had seen. Compared to what she'd been through, they sheltered me. But I was still determined to win here and prove to her I could fight if I had to.

Heck, I planned to do a lot more than win educationally in this place, if any of my fellow students turned out to be worth dating. With this welcome, they looked like a gang of internet trolls—not worth my time. But I couldn't let a loud minority shape my view of the school too much.

We drove around the packed parking lot, searching for a space, while Mom perched at the wheel with her hands white-knuckled around it. "If you tell me you will be all right, I will try to trust you. But I do not trust the men who think they own every inch of this place. It was the school's decision. The men should accept it, but they do not."

"No, they don't," I sighed as we drove down the next aisle of cars. "Some of them are being big babies about it."

Being the first female student on a traditionally all-male campus would not be easy. I was tough, but with all the anger online, the alums queuing up to talk about what a shame it was to let a woman into the university and treating me like a marauding invader, the hateful emails I had received, the dirt-digging journalists I had dealt with...none of it felt good.

No matter what the stupid boys crowding the front entrance thought, no matter what they accused, I wasn't doing this to make some kind of feminist statement.

I wasn't doing it for publicity, to carve out space for women, to spite men, or to violate a sexist tradition.

I was here because of the scholarship, the quality of the school, and what I wanted to do with my life.

This school's journalism program was one of the best in the country, and the scholarship was the only way I could get into anything resembling its caliber. So, I had gone for it—and succeeded. Any other details or motivations took a distant second to that.

"Babies can't hurt you." Mom touched her earlobe unconsciously, toying with a small scar. "Unless they grab your earrings," she teased, trying to break the tense mood. I rolled my eyes, and she smiled briefly.

With a tired wariness, I wondered whether the boys would

remember there was a second entrance to the dorms and come running around bothering us while we were unpacking the car. I wouldn't put it past them. After all those hysterical rants about how men were being "robbed" of their private spaces, there was very little they wouldn't do.

But Mom was forgetting a few things—like my ability to defend myself, how hard it was to intimidate me after growing up in Hell's Kitchen, and how little I cared about some spoiled boys' assessment of me. I wasn't here to rob them of anything. I had earned my place there with a full scholarship, outdoing every single male applicant with no extra help. If they really had wanted to keep me out, they should have studied harder. I was a little worried about the destructive tantrums of dyed-in-the-wool sexists and neurotic "activists" mobilizing in defense of male privilege, but not impressed by the guys involved to fear them long term.

For now, I wanted to get my crap upstairs and into my single dorm room, so Mom could drive away from this uncomfortable situation and I could get a damn nap. Driving from Hellbender, New York, down to the tip of Long Island had taken it out of me. I just hoped Mom could make her way back all right. At least it was still early.

I had two suitcases, one achingly heavy from my books, and an additional box full of groceries and drinks that Mom had pressed on me and refused to take back. She didn't trust the cafeteria system, believing they served nothing but junk. Good thing I had sprung for a dorm fridge and that there was a kitchen on each floor.

"Don't let those boys take your food either," Mom warned me as she reached behind her seat and pulled out one of my suitcases. "I paid good money for it."

"I won't." I was sure I could probably get a halfway decent meal at the cafeteria, but that didn't mean I didn't want other options. Hopefully, all these angry "advocates" wouldn't throw a fit over my using the dorm kitchen. "Mama, are you going to be all right up on that mountain by yourself?"

"I'll be fine. I've got the dogs, and Mrs. Avery and I will eat supper together." She squinted slightly with affection. "Don't you worry about me. You worry about yourself. Keep up your studies. Call me." She finished unloading everything, and I grabbed the box and the other suitcase, turning to face the tall stucco building while she locked up.

They had set me up in a corner single suite on the fourth floor, with a private bathroom. It was a setup used for disabled kids who needed accessibility, but my special need was having a shower to myself. Mom had made sure, by raising hell about the administration wanting me to use communal bathrooms or showers, and she had threatened to leak their proposal to the press. I was glad she did. The last thing I needed was to deal with showering where some guy had left behind a hidden camera.

"I'm going to call regularly," I promised gently as I shouldered the box and dragged the suitcase along. I took after Dad more, taller, athletic, less timid. I had taken over jar-opening and grocery-carrying duty since his death and now balanced the heavy box on my shoulder with practiced grace.

She moved ahead and pushed the lobby door open for us—only to stop short, confronted by some sign-waving men who had piled into the space and were blocking the elevators. "Oh," she said and muttered something in Kreyol that I didn't catch. I could hear the fear in her voice. I wasn't having it. *You don't get to scare my mom.* I moved ahead of her, studying the knot of men.

Most of them were young—incoming freshmen or close to it, with sloppy T-shirts, snapbacks, hoodies, early fall versions of skater clothes. Still high school boys, really, complete with obvious cool-guy loathing of any girl they couldn't get their dicks in.

They smirked at me with bully delight, while a red-faced guy with at least ten years on them pushed to the front of the group.

"You thought you could go around us," he sneered as I took him in coldly. I could hear Mom hesitating behind me, worried about the potential confrontation. Meanwhile, I was assessing him and them.

The main aggressor, Mr. Perpetual Student, was a big, messy slouch of a man with an unkempt russet beard and the pasty skin of someone who lived his whole life indoors. A stale smell of junk food and cigarettes rolled off his black overcoat.

"Well, think again!" He started up his pretentious speech again while I stared at him. Some guys around us shifted restlessly, as if starting to realize their banner-bearer was off his damn rocker over nothing. Two of them started snickering at him. He seemed oblivious, puffing himself up and folding his arms. "I won't allow you to defile this campus with your—"

"With what, my cooties?" I challenged him. "Grow up."

More nervous laughter from the crowd—mixed with a deep-voiced chuckle that briefly distracted me into investigating its source. Then I stared back at Mr. Perpetual Student, watching him huff while his face turned purple. "You have no right to be here!" he yelled.

"That's not your call. Get the fuck out of the way," I said tiredly.

He blinked in shock at my unladylike language as a few guys chuckled and moved back, but the rest folded their arms, still smirking. Out of the corner of my eye, I saw a figure in a black leather jacket just leaning against the wall, watching the fun.

"Make me!" His voice quavered childishly.

I stared at him for a second, then shrugged, set down the suitcase, and pulled out my phone.

His eyes widened, and he took a half step backward. "What —who are you calling?" he demanded suspiciously.

I shrugged my free shoulder. "Campus security. They find out you're blocking students from entering the dorm, you'll probably spend a chunk of time in a cell."

He swallowed, the red draining from his face. "You wouldn't."

"You bet your ass, I would," I declared, glaring at him hard as I took a half step forward. "See, I don't give a shit about your hurt ego or your problems with women or your need to throw all that weight around. That's not my concern. You, your anger, all this bullshit, these teenage boys you've rallied to your little hateful cause..." I swept my arm around to take in the remaining guys. "None of that fucking shit matters to me."

"This is men's space—" he started, but I just shook my head.

"This is the school where I have a full-ride scholarship. The administration decided that this is no longer 'men's space,' not me. They offered me the ride. I took it. There is nothing more to it than that." I continued staring hard at him, my eyes aching and my heart pounding from the social discomfort but determined to make my point. "If you have a problem with that, take it up with the administration or go whine about it in your hate groups online. Because I don't care."

The guy went pale as another whooped. I heard the door open as some of his backup left. He turned to watch them go, then turned back and gave me a panicked stare.

"Make yourself scarce," I advised, hovering my thumb over my phone's touchscreen. "Or you can get kicked out for causing trouble and relive your youth at another goddamn campus."

His lips trembled as he glanced from me to Mom to his

dwindling support, until finally, he eyed me and stumbled for the far door. Two guys laughed at him as he passed.

I scooped my suitcase up again and glanced back at Mom, who was staring at me wide-eyed. "Oh my God, child," she said and then laughed and shook her head. "What have I raised?"

"A fighter, Mama." I walked up to the elevator doors and pressed the button to summon it.

"That was a little dangerous. I don't think he had his head on properly." Mom dragged my suitcase through the elevator door when it came, scowling with worry.

"I didn't mean to upset you, Mama, but I had to do something. He was going to keep talking and making a fuss until I did." I carted the rest of my stuff in and then leaned against the wall beside her, facing outward. "Guys like that don't stop until you push back."

There were still a few guys in the lobby, including the one in the black leather jacket, one arm folded over his broad chest as he talked on the phone. He examined me. Our eyes met just as the door closed, giving me a glimpse of pale irises the color of silver coins. Then the doors slammed shut.

"Just be careful, child. Too many of these women-hating men are shooting up places these days." *My poor mom.* I could still see the fear in her dark eyes at the thought of my being here alone.

"I will be," I promised, but mostly, I was just pissed off. I didn't really care if a bunch of assholes wanted to throw their little tantrums and make my life less convenient. They would soon learn that I was just another student and didn't give a damn about the political uproar, or they would get security called on them and get tossed out of school.

There was nobody in the hallway when we got upstairs. We made our way to the small door at the end of the hall. I snatched the folded note taped to the door off it before Mom caught up, and I tried my key.

The room within was small and plain, with dark gray office carpet, a long, narrow bed, a desk, and a single large window. Unadorned white walls. Thin horizontal blinds. The bathroom beyond its open door was barely larger than the closet. I crossed to the window and peered out, watching the guys who had been bothering us walk away across the quad in front of the dormitory. One of them tossed his sign in the trash as he went.

"This looks all right." Mom set down the suitcase of books with a sigh, and I placed the box of food on the desk. "At least they did not make you have roommates."

"No way I would put up with that," I sighed, poking through the small chest of drawers tucked inside the closet. "Not really any room for over one suitcase."

"I'll take back the other one for now." Mom put her fists on her hips and scanned around the room, then stared back up at me with soft-eyed worry. "I don't want to leave you here alone."

"I know." I gave her a firm hug, smelling her vetiver perfume, and sighed into her close-cropped hair. "I'll call every day if it makes you feel better."

She lingered a little while as I unpacked my books from the suitcase and piled them on my bed and desk. I had gotten my books early via mail order to get a jump on reading them. The journalists' biographies tempted me to open them and resume reading instead of putting them away. But she needed to get back home before dark, so I resisted and laid them aside with the others.

Finally, we said our goodbyes, and she walked back out to the truck and left. I returned to my dorm room, sat down on my bed, and sighed. *I made it. I'm here. They didn't stop me.*

I reached into my pocket and pulled out the crumpled note. I unfolded it and studied the single word scrawled on it in

Sharpie. The men of Markinswell had decided how they would represent themselves to me, Mom, the administration, and the public. It seemed some of them would have to face consequences before they would back down. Maybe a little public humiliation was in order.

I got my dorm room cleaned up first. Clothes hung up, the bureau stuffed full of books, my suitcase tucked under my bed. Food arranged on top of the bureau if it didn't go in the fridge. Chair against the door with its back tucked under the knob. Then I took a long shower. Back home, fuel oil was precious. Showers were down to four minutes, twice that if I needed to wash my hair. Here, someone else was footing the bill, so I took my time scrubbing and washing my thick mahogany-brown curls. It took me a while to dry and style my hair while standing in the warm, steamy room. But I definitely wanted to get my appearance right before I went on camera.

I glanced at the note again as I was getting dressed in one of my few nice, corporate-looking outfits. The silvery tweed popped against my dark skin. The careful bun made me appear older, more respectable. Makeup and jewelry, nice but not too flashy. I looked professional and grown-up.

In short, I looked way better than the guys trying to block my entrance or leaving obscenities on my door. And I was about to make sure that many people saw that.

With enough negative reinforcement, they would likely stop. And if not, well, I would have plenty of documentation to bring to the administration. Whatever happened, whatever they tried, I wasn't letting the bastards on campus impede my education.

CHAPTER 2

SABINE

"TWO HUNDRED THOUSAND VIEWS SO FAR," I murmured proudly as I sat back from my desk a week later. "Not bad. Not bad at all."

School had started, and I was slowly getting into the swing of things. After days of working at it, I was finally settling into a routine that wasn't all about dealing with salty boys. It still partly was, but not so much that I felt overwhelmed. Then again, it took a lot to overwhelm me.

My classes were tough. Eighteen units in my first semester, my first class at eight in the morning, another one running until seven at night. I'd sorted out all the details, from where everything was on campus, to dining hall credits, to where to do my laundry, to the fact that I had to stay there and watch said laundry to avoid coming back to discover some pervert up to his elbows in it. That had happened two days ago. The guy in question, a little weasel of a freshman boy with pasty skin and cowlicked blond hair, had straightened up quickly with a fistful of my panties and an expression of panic on his face. I had recorded him on my phone, while demanding to know what he was doing, why he was touching my underwear, why his pants were unbuckled and unzipped, what his name was, and what his parents would think when I published this without blurring out his face.

He had tried threatening me at first until I had mentioned that I was live-streaming to a friend and she was recording. I had been sweating through it underneath the bravado, because I had been bullshitting about the live stream. There had been no time to set it up.

Fortunately, he was scared and embarrassed and, apparently, rather stupid. All the rage had drained out of him, and he had cowered away from the phone like a vampire from a cross. Exposure really was the absolute best weapon to use against bastards like him. He had obediently tossed the panties back into the wash on my demand. Then he had blubbered and begged. I had stood firm, warning him coldly that I would publish and tell the administration the second he gave me any more trouble. Once I had gotten him bobbing his head in desperate acknowledgment of his understanding, I had let him run. Stayed composed. Finished my laundry. Hand-washing those panties in the sink three times. After that, I'd gone back to my dorm room and propped the extra chair I had borrowed from the common room under my doorknob again.

Mom didn't know about the pervert panty-thief. She didn't know about the men who had tried to block my way, the ones who had knocked my books from my hands, those who had smeared my seat with paint or tried to shout me down in class. I hadn't reported any incidents beyond the first day to her, or on my blog, which was published weekly right now while I settled in.

But I had recorded the incidents. Every one of them. And everyone causing me problems had gotten nervous and backed down, because I had already shown them I would use my journalistic skills against them at the drop of a fucking hat.

I needed an income, though, because if I kept using my phone on people, they would soon try to break or steal it. I would need a dedicated camera, one for the peephole in my door, and a concealed one I would wear. I had declared that I was always recording and that I now had someone off campus involved—my "editor," who received the streams. I was editing my stuff, but they didn't need to know I didn't have any backup. In fact, it was important that they didn't.

Maybe I should monetize my blog? But not with ads. I'd just add a donation button. I had resisted the idea for a long while, mostly because I had been raised not to take charity. But there were plenty of "buy me a coffee" level donation sites that bothered me less to use. *Yeah, I'll do that.*

Markinswell's faculty, staff, and administration didn't appreciate my publishing my negative experiences online. The day after I had published my first piece, they had called me into the assistant dean of journalism's office and asked me to take it down. I had agreed—if I went a solid week without being harassed.

The assistant dean, a small, mousy man with black hair that looked like a layer of shellac, had given me a frightened stare, protesting that they couldn't stop "boys from being boys."

I'd smiled and told him I would not be complicit in hiding my harassment so they could maintain a facade of respectability without being respectable.

That had shocked him into silence. I didn't know if it had been my audacity or my words, but I had finally broken through to him. I was very serious.

I had patiently explained to him that I had come here expecting to create a positive blog about the educational experience they had offered me. If my experience was overall negative, however, that was impossible without outright lying.

It was their idea to open the campus to women, to offer me this scholarship, and to promise me I would be safe here. It was their obligation to prevent any student from being harassed, and that they had created a bigger job for themselves where I was concerned did not change that. If their reputation suffered because a loud minority of boys threw a fit and they did nothing to predict, manage, or contain it, it was their fault.

I had also asked him if I could get his cease and desist request in writing so I could send a copy to my lawyer.

He had backed down after that, and instead, consequences had finally started happening.

A security camera in my hallway had stopped the notes on my door and the random banging in the middle of the night. Professors had embarrassed the worst of them in class. One or two persistent idiots had gotten thrown out of my English class altogether. My forwarding threatening emails to faculty and administration, and to one or two mothers, had slowed them to a trickle.

But nothing had made more impact than the vlog post the assistant dean wanted so badly to be taken down, because it had gone viral—thanks to the tantrums and threats thrown around in the comments. By trying to harass me into silence, those same boys had confirmed my stories of harassment.

I played that video again, narrowing my eyes slightly as I critiqued my work. I needed to use a little more hair oil before going on camera. My hair got all frizzy from the dorm room being steamy. Cute, but not professional enough. My makeup was on point, forest-green liner bringing out the red and gold tones in my bright brown eyes, and my confident smile didn't waver.

"Good afternoon, everyone. This is Sabine here with

Adventures at Markinswell. It's my first day here. I just got dropped off at my dorm by my mom and have gotten everything set up. As I promised, I'm checking in as soon as possible after arriving." I beamed at the camera—actually just my phone on a tripod sitting in my closet on top of the bureau. It had done the trick, thank God.

In the video, I sat in my chair with my laptop open and the monitor on, displaying as many of the hateful and threatening emails I had received as would fit on my screen. I taped the note to the wall beside the screen, proudly displaying its single word:

CUNT

And yet I smiled like nothing was wrong as I went on.

"The weather's lovely here, a nippy fifty-eight degrees." The screen switched to the photos I had taken on the way, the trees, monuments, buildings, and the angry crowd. I included that last one without comment, letting it pique my viewers' curiosity before explaining it. "Fall colors are perfect, and the campus is beautiful. I'm scheduled for eighteen units this semester. It worried some of you that I would overtax myself between school, the blog, and visits upstate, but I promise, I'm doing fine. Also, one of my professors is apparently a Pulitzer Prize winner. I'll search for the details for you and add them in the comment section. I'm so excited to be here!"

In the video's background, someone started pounding on the door. I managed not to jump. My smile died, and I sat patiently as the banging drowned out everything else.

"Come on out, slut. I want a blow job." Three male voices laughed, then more banging. "Come on! You know that's why you came here to be around all these guys—you're a straight-up cock-hungry whore, so give it up."

I kept my composure. "Unfortunately, while the maples

and aspens all over campus have been showing their colors, so have the delightful men of the Markinswell student body."

More banging. "Come on and suck it, slut!"

On-screen, I smiled tightly. "Their response to the administrative decision to allow women to enroll as students has not been taken to the administration. Instead, it is being brought to me."

More banging.

I spoke a little louder, making my words very clear. "Even before I arrived" —the screen switched to a close-up of the threatening emails— "they made it clear that not only I am not welcome, but that a significant number of them are men no woman would want to be around."

The banging halted. "Dude," a male voice hissed audibly. "I think she's recording this or something."

I stifled a laugh. The few seconds where their conversation was recorded was definitely the best part.

"Shit," muttered the first boy. All his bravado faded fast. "Let's get the fuck out of here."

My stage smile went a little more genuine as the feed switched back to me, and the insult still glared from the paper on the wall, its significance unmistakable now. I didn't have to go off about finding it on my door. I didn't have to explain the emails. I didn't have to tell them that repulsive bullies had been banging on my door and yelling through it like that for hours off and on. All the evidence was right there for them to hear and see—thanks to the timely idiots who had dropped by to demonstrate.

"I've made it very clear from the beginning that my sole goal for being at Markinswell is academic achievement. That is what I will continue to pursue, despite all this..." I glanced back at the sign and smiled sweetly at the camera. "...pushback."

Somebody kicked my door hard enough to make the chair

propped against it shake. On the screen, my composure wavered.

"As for a bunch of insecure guys who think the best way to maintain their boys' club is to drive me away, even if they could, this was an administrative decision. I'm not trespassing." I sighed, then put a small, polite smile back on. "I never advocated for Markinswell to become co-ed. I couldn't care less that male-only colleges exist or that female-only colleges exist. All I did was pursue the best educational opportunity available to me. The whole debate should be with the administration."

Someone started rattling the door handle. They stopped after a few seconds, and my smile briefly wobbled. I was crumpling in front of the camera—just a little, but enough that I could see the stress. And so could my viewers. And that was half the point, so I didn't care if it made me appear a little unprofessional.

On video, I lifted my chin confidently. "But I'm not going anywhere. Instead, I'm going to document everything. Every harassment, every theft, every death threat, every nasty note, everything. What I do after that depends on how I'm treated." For a second, my smile faded, and I stared into the camera, then I turned it back on like I had flipped a switch.

"But enough about that. It's not as if every guy in this place feels threatened that one member of their class isn't male. Anyway, they should feel a lot more threatened that I'm going to ruin their grade curve. Which I will." I winked at the camera.

I stopped the video and glanced down at the comments again. I'd deleted many after I had followed up on some non-anonymous death threats, but I had already documented everything. From what I had seen so far, it was only about five percent of the student body that had any obvious problems with my presence. Of those, only about a quarter seemed like I would need to report them. The only problem was, that was over sixty students, some of whom I shared classes with. *Am I really going to take that many idiots to the brink of expulsion before they will back down? That will eat up all my time. I can't afford it.*

I was puzzling out that problem when I heard a much more polite tapping on the door. "Hey, sweetie. It's Billy. Are you in?"

I smiled. Billy lived two doors down and had been getting the business too, though not quite as badly. He and I, and a few others from the scholarship crowd, had banded together quickly—mostly to have someone friendly to eat meals with and talk about the school situation.

I opened the door. Billy reminded me of my favorite Spider-Man—small, slim, with big brown eyes, medium-length natural hair, and a preference for hoodies. "Hi!" he exclaimed brightly as he bustled in carrying a grocery bag.

"Hey, little bro. How did your day go?" He got a hug. He smelled faintly of weed.

"Oh, today was my short day, so I went out to the apple festival." He produced an overfilled bag of apples and a jar of apple butter. "I love fall."

"I'm going to get so fat if you keep doing this," I mock-wailed as I gratefully stuck the apple butter in my little fridge.

He just laughed. "You're fine, sweetie, you're fine. How are things going since you talked to the assistant dean?"

I noticed him eyeing my screen, and my smile went rueful. "They're more interested in preserving the school's reputation than anything else. I told them I would stop reporting on their students being shitty to me when there was nothing to report." I quirked up one corner of my mouth. "It's put a dent in their bullshit already."

"Good! I'm sick of them getting away with this crap. What

about Panty Raid?" Billy was one of only two people I had told about the creepy blond in the laundry room.

"He seems to have vanished off the face of the planet. Maybe he dropped out. Good thing if he did." I shuddered as I remembered his skinny fingers plucking greedily at the lace edge of my favorite boy shorts.

"Yeah, well, I see a guy who looks like that in this building, I'll follow him to his room and let you know." He shook his head in disgust. "You should blackmail him or something."

I scoffed in agreement, but inside, I felt sad and worried. I always did these days. Even if only a small chunk of the student body hated me and wanted me gone, I didn't always know which of these guys would pop up and turn out to be one of them.

I had gotten every kind of guy pissed at me for being here and female—older students, guys a few months younger than me, rich, here on scholarship, conservative, nominally liberal, arts students, business students, journalism students. And the animosity toward me was going to make it tough to date. So much so, in fact, that my original hopes of finding an on-campus boyfriend were down the toilet.

"Their straightness isn't the problem. Their dedication to hating the same people they want to fuck is." And that was the thing. These guys, like the creep with the panties, the assholes who had pounded on my door, or the furious ball of body hair and stink that I had met down in the lobby, had no problem sexualizing me. But they didn't seem able to view me as human.

"And that's how you get bullies." Billy chuckled and fished out an apple for himself from the bag.

"Yep." I sighed. "It's also how you get me wary of dating while I'm here. At least dating a fellow student."

"Oh, you don't want to date a Markinswell guy anyway. They're all trash. Trust me, I've tried it." He waved a hand dismissively before sitting down in my spare chair and taking a huge bite of his apple. "Spoiled rich boys give shitty dick game."

I laughed. "Billy."

"It's true, though!" He gave me a wide-eyed innocent stare, and I chuckled more. He shook his head. "Seriously. Date off campus. You'll be a lot happier."

Well, that would solve my problem. "You may be right." I walked over to the window and peered at the quad beyond the small parking lot, full of guys hurrying back and forth. "Almost nobody on campus shows much promise anyway."

Though that wasn't true. There were those guys, the ones I almost always saw together when I ran across them between classes. I called them the Alpha Omega guys because they wore their fraternity jackets or their pins everywhere they went. They were also noticeable for how the students and faculty treated them.

Respectfully. Almost deferential. Crowds parting for them. Guys hurrying up to them with eager questions. It was clear. If I was a pariah on campus thanks to all the sexism, these guys were the rock stars. And every one of them was hot as the road surface on a July afternoon.

"Do you know anything about Alpha Omega?" I asked quietly as I watched the guys walk back and forth.

I heard some slow, thoughtful munching, then a swallow. "Big men on campus," Billy sighed. "Hot, high grades, all the connections, and way too straight. Five inner circle members— they call them the Gentlemen's Club—plus maybe a dozen lower-level members and a bunch of pledges."

I eyed him, lifting an eyebrow. It would be just my luck to find myself attracted to a bunch of spoiled frat boys. A dark-haired one with gray eyes. A black-haired one with really pale skin and black eyes. Two beefy blonds, one hazel-eyed and towering, the other blue-eyed and more normal-sized. And a lanky one with auburn hair and a serious face. A whole damn box of man candy is what they were, and I was sure they were aware of it. None of them had ever antagonized me or had ever even spoken to me. But every time I was in the same vicinity as them, I caught them watching me, and I didn't know whether to be flattered or worried.

Maybe both.

Billy's jaw dropped as he saw my thoughtful expression. "You're not getting a crush on any of them, right?"

Any? No.

But I'd probably say yes to a date with any of them if they turned out not to be assholes.

"No," I reassured him firmly. "You're right. I should find someone off campus to date."

"Well, good. Because they go through women like razors, and I'm sure you don't want to be that type of girl."

What he meant was disposable.

I nodded, hearing him loud and clear. "No," I insisted firmly. "Definitely not."

CHAPTER 3

BLAKE

"WELL, are you going to do something about that bitch or what?" Mikey Carmody shifted from one battered jump boot to the other impatiently, his voice rising to an irritating whine.

I stayed where I was on the couch in our downstairs common room, staring at the perpetual pledge with strained patience. Carmody was twenty-nine years old, the oldest student on campus and, arguably, the least mature. He had ten years on some of my companions in the room, but he often acted like a small child who was being denied ice cream.

Around the room, I heard several faint chuckles. Half the fraternity was hanging around after the barbecue to shoot pool, drink beer, and play video games. In the middle of our relaxation, and much to my annoyance, Carmody had used them as a captive audience while he unloaded his complaints to me —again.

"Something is being done," I countered. He blinked at me dully. Carmody had a tendency to misinterpret everything that we senior fraternity members told him, or forget he was told and then come complaining to us with the same problem again.

He was the absolute worst part of leading the fraternity, and I genuinely wished he would either graduate or possibly leave the planet.

Meanwhile, I spoke slowly and used small words while, beside me, my cousin Marcus recorded the entire conversation. Playing the conversations we had back to thickheaded Carmody helped make sure he either remembered what we were talking about or was set straight if he insisted on being an ass. "I said this yesterday, Carmody. Try to pay attention this time."

He puffed out his cheeks and fidgeted, reddening more.

I studied him with a bored expression until he settled down.

"What?" Carmody asked. "What did you say?"

"I said that we would handle the Sabine Keegan problem by ourselves. We need no further intervention or help on your part. Do not approach her again. The matter is well in hand." His expression crumpled, and I braced myself to wrestle with the urge to punch his face in. "I said it is well in hand, Carmody."

"But—" he started.

I lifted an eyebrow.

He started harrumphing and shuffling more, as if working up all his nerves. "She's still here! You said you'd make her go."

"These things take time and subtlety to execute correctly. What are you expecting me to do, put a hit out on the girl because the faculty made a decision you don't agree with since you hate women?" I asked him in a very bored tone.

He looked like he was about to suggest it.

Jesus fucking Christ, this guy needs either a good therapist or a good cage, and I'm not sure which one.

"Don't even answer that," I instructed, and he sagged a little.

Beside me, Marcus snickered.

I continued, "Buddy, you cannot reverse the administration's decision by driving out one woman. Besides, she's their political pawn."

"Then we have to drive out all the women!" Carmody cried with so much malicious zeal, I wondered if he was just straight-up crazy. "Just knock all their pawns off the board."

Oh my God, what the hell is wrong with this guy? Besides him being a nearly thirty-year-old sophomore.

I uncrossed my arms, sat forward, and steepled my fingers, my eyes hard on Carmody's. "Shut. Up!"

Worried muttering came from around the room. Carmody's mouth closed with a meaty noise, and he blinked at me mutely.

"That's better." I tapped my fingertips together. "When you and the other pledges came to us and asked us to discourage Sabine Keegan from continuing at this school, the five of us agreed to look into the matter. We are doing so. If you continue to distract us—and question our authority and judgment with your constant pestering—you not only slow this process down, you place your status as a pledge in jeopardy."

Carmody went pale. "I didn't realize."

"No. You didn't think," I corrected. "You spend too much time emoting. To be honest, most men in this institution wouldn't suffer one bit for having a pretty face around." There was chuckling and nodding around the room. "But that doesn't mean we should turn a deaf ear to those concerned about this situation with Sabine. And we have not."

Down the couch from me, Daniel, one of my fellow Gentlemen's Club members, stifled a chuckle and shook his blond-spiked head before saying in his slight German accent, "You do not make a request of us and then expect us to wave our hands at your behest. Blake is correct. This is not a simple matter of frightening the poor girl off. It needs to at least appear to be her decision. Sabine is a pawn of the administration. Were it not her, it would be someone else. A personal vendetta against the girl is pointless."

Carmody's jaw dropped. "But..."

"They will replace her if we do that, Carmody," I pointed out. "If our interference is exposed, ultimately, the only ones who will lose face will be us."

"Then..." Carmody peered around at all of us, strangely baffled and hurt, as if he had never figured out how the world worked while being coddled by his wealthy parents. "Then how do we get our school back?"

"Sabine is a means to their end." Nathaniel's solemn voice from down at the end of the table caught everyone's attention. He rarely said anything unless it was important.

I interjected, "And their endgame is making this a coeducational university. We don't want that to happen." I arched a brow. "But the administration has ignored both us and their major donors."

"Major donors?" Marcus chuckled. "Just say our parents, Blake. Carmody's too, or he wouldn't even be here."

The corner of my eye twitched. "We do not, as we've all learned, control the opinions or actions of our parents. They share our interest in maintaining a single-sex campus. They also, like you, Carmody, believe that the distraction of women will prevent us from focusing on our studies."

"And what a lovely distraction she is," Daniel commented cheerfully.

There were chuckles around the room, except for Carmody, whose face matched his ratty purple sweater. If there was one thing Carmody hated more than women, it was the reminder that most of us didn't share his hatred.

Damn, now I have to settle them down before he has a stroke or something.

"Braun, you're not helping."

Marcus laughed and patted my shoulder. "Lighten up, cousin. You know we all think so." His eyes twinkled, and I shrugged in response.

"Fine," I grumbled. He was correct. Sabine was exquisite. Her beauty, like her fire, lingered in my memory even when I didn't want it to. Dark eyes, fluffy, tousled hair, courage, and grace. We had been watching her from afar, and her poise under the stress of this situation was attractive. In other circumstances, I would have planned to get her into my bed, not drive her out of Markinswell. *Hmm. Perhaps I can do both.*

"I have nothing personal against the girl," I stated. "She's poor, and this seems to be her one shot at a prestigious university like Markinswell." I let that point sink in. I saw a lot of uncomfortable fidgeting around the room.

I needed something stronger than the drink in my hand. All this friction was leaving a foul taste in my mouth. But I couldn't ignore the needs of my pledges, even if some of them were being idiots about this Sabine clusterfuck.

I continued, "If we drive her away with harassment that she can document and report, we'll be expelled, and another girl will replace her. If she leaves voluntarily, for something unrelated to us, with no documentation implicating anyone, it will look like her own failure. That will make her an embarrassment to the university and strengthen our position."

Carmody blinked as he digested my words. "So, you're planning something subtle."

Oh dear God, you are about five steps behind.

Can we get rid of you instead?

I stared at him until he fidgeted again. "Yes. Exactly. If you don't ruin it with your lack of couth."

Carmody relaxed a little. His nervous smile told me that

even he knew better than to press his luck any further. "I'll stay away from her. Just as long as you're acting on this."

I stomped on my surge of anger and lifted an eyebrow coldly. He turned and hurried out, mumbling his farewells over his shoulder.

I puffed out my breath in relief as he left. The newer members were all drifting away now that the show was over, leaving the five of us lounging around with our beers.

"So, what do you plan to do?" Jude, the shortest and youngest of us, tossed his blond mop off his forehead and stared at me with interest. He was the one the pledges had come to. He had the closest ties to them and listened to them a little too much. Of the five in our inner circle, he was the one I felt needed the closest watching. He was empathetic but emotional, and a touch immature.

I took a sip of my beer. "Well, I've given it some thought. We need more information on our girl, so we can assess her weaknesses and personality traits. So far, she seems both highly intelligent and very strong-willed. And she has no qualms about damaging the reputations of those who harm her by exposing them."

"How do you plan to avoid her trying that on us?" Nathaniel asked, tilting his head slightly. "She's a reporter. She's already using her skills as her best weapon against her tormentors."

"Well..." I smirked. "Remember how you're always referring to emotions as a weakness?"

I heard a rustle as the guys sat forward in their seats and turned to me, suddenly very interested. Nathaniel stayed perfectly still, narrow white hands folded in his lap, and lifted an eyebrow. "Yes?" he queried.

"The best way to get the administration's pawn to leave is willingly, discreetly," I started. "And without the ability to think about the situation. What if she were to have her heart broken, multiple times in quick succession, by men she thinks she has something special with?"

Jude whooped with approval.

Nathaniel sat back, frowning thoughtfully.

Marcus sat quietly with his brows drawn together. "That's kind of cruel," he protested, surprising me a little. He was usually the first to make a joke, even in tense circumstances.

I nodded. "Cruel but necessary. Go too hard, and we'll all end up in trouble. But go too gently, and she won't leave." And she needed to leave. The uproar over her was too disruptive. It wasn't like I could go around duct-taping the mouths of every Carmody on campus. There had to be over sixty of them, as embarrassing as it was to admit that.

But Marcus, of all of us, didn't seem entirely on board. "Is there something you'd like to say, Marcus?" I asked gently.

Marcus shook his head. "If you say it's necessary, I believe you. But I wish there were a different way."

"Well, let's discuss that," I challenged, biting back my irritation. "What would you suggest? Bribery?"

"If I thought she'd go along with that, yes," Marcus affirmed. "The five of us could pay her way through to a doctorate at any school in the country on less than our investments together make in a month. We wouldn't even require help from our parents anymore."

I pressed my lips together. If I were honest with myself, I would have preferred something that simple. But Marcus's reluctance in the face of obvious necessity bothered me.

"I would not be against such a plan," I countered. "If we could be certain it would work."

Nathaniel uncoiled from his tense posture, stretching his long limbs. "It won't." His eyes hooded thoughtfully. "We should have tried that plan a few weeks ago, prior to the backlash. But now, the blundering of men like Carmody has angered her. Her guard is up. If we approach her with a bribery attempt, we'll likely end up internet famous for it. The risk is too great."

I peered at Marcus, who slowly nodded and sat back, conceding.

I glanced around. "Any other protest against my plan?"

"So, your plan is that we all date and fuck her, then all dump her?" Daniel lifted an eyebrow. "Do we do this in any order, or...?"

"No, let's tempt her into something more scandalous." I smiled lopsidedly. "We'll share her and leave her torn between us. Whoever she confesses to first breaks up with her first."

Quiet spread over our little group. I could tell the other four were interested, but like me, they were debating.

"What are you going to do if she's a one-guy woman?" Marcus still sounded troubled. "Most women aren't interested in dating five guys at once."

I shrugged. "Same plan, but in serial instead of at once. One of us dumps her, the rest court her on the rebound, drop her again, and so on." I held up an imperious finger. "Gentlemen, I'm talking about pulling out all the stops here. Whirlwind romance. Gifts, charm, seduction, the works. Make her believe it."

Nathaniel leaned back and propped his hands behind his head. "Raise her up on an emotional high, while tempting her into scandalous behavior that will prevent her from reporting us for fear of losing her own reputation."

"Who gets her virginity?" Daniel asked casually, as if he were finding out who was picking up the tab for pizza. "I have never seen such an obvious virgin in my life. Was she born with a textbook in her hands?"

Marcus shot him a stare so dirty that for a moment, it

looked like he was going to walk out. But then, he glanced back at me and calmed down, saying nothing.

"If she is a virgin, obviously the answer is whomever of us she surrenders to first." I wanted it to be me, but I didn't say that. If they knew how attracted to Sabine I really was, they would question my impartiality. That couldn't happen. Instead, I smiled mildly and took a swallow of my beer. "May the best seducer win."

Everyone was nodding, expressions amused, except for thoughtful Marcus and Nathaniel, who still looked like he was doing math equations in his head. Sometimes I wondered if that weird, detached fucker ever got excited over anything.

"Okay," Marcus drawled. "So, who breaks the ice with her?"

I smirked. "Oh, that's easy. It's my idea, so I'll do it and let you all know how it goes."

Daniel chuckled and shook his head. "Good luck, man. If she sniffs you out, the entire game is over before it begins."

CHAPTER 4

BLAKE

I PUT my plan into motion immediately.

Sabine and I shared two classes, English literature survey and a small panel on journalistic ethics. The first was so enormous that I could watch her from the crowd, the class held in a cavernous auditorium. The second was in a small classroom that reminded me of high school. A much better choice for what I was planning. There, I would try to engage with her through the back-and-forth of class discussion.

The first week of classes had involved massive disruptions from the same fifty-odd angry young men who shared any classes or space with Sabine. I had watched the pranks, the harassment, the outright threats. I had seen her hair pulled, her clothes grabbed, and three attempts at up her skirt photos that had her wearing long skirts and trousers now. She was showing all the poise of a professional journalist dealing with an unpleasant assignment, but she had to be suffering under the surface.

Watching her in English from a few rows behind, I marveled at how tough she was. The men after her had been weeded out now or forced to quiet down, but they still challenged everything she said in class. Yet she held up every single time.

I sipped my latte, watching as a fellow student spluttered through an attempt to decimate her academically.

"I strongly disagree with Sabine's point," the pseudo-academic in the cartoon T-shirt spoke up almost shrilly. "There's absolutely no evidence that Sethe had to sleep with the stonemason to pay for her child's gravestone in *Beloved*. Not one line even hints at that."

The professor, a gigantic bear of a guy who looked like he might moonlight as a mall Santa, rolled his eyes and sighed, and an uncomfortable chuckle ran through the crowd. The guy was dead wrong, but about eighty percent of the time with these guys, that was true. Sabine was smart and well-read, and her detractors spent more energy on hating her than they did on intelligently refuting her arguments.

Sabine stood. "With Professor Gomez's permission, I'd like to read from the text." He nodded assent as the chuckling grew louder. "Chapter one, pages thirteen to fourteen." She sat there reading through the quote, as calmly as if reading it off for her news vlog. By the end, her challenger had gone from smug to red to white to sweating in embarrassment.

Mic drop. More laughter rippled as the guy flopped back into his seat. I sneered at the back of his head. *Childish.* This behavior damaged our reputations, not her reporting on it.

Professor Gomez took it from there as Sabine sat down, her challenger silenced. "As you can see from this passage, Sethe suffers a flashback of what she had to do to pay for her baby's gravestone. This was very much a traumatic event for her, not only because of her blood guilt about her baby, but because she had to degrade herself sexually just to pay for aspects of her baby's funeral. In this flashback, there are two Sethes. The grieving mother who wants to honor her child, and the child-killer, obviously suicidal, who is doing penance for her crime. And as we see in her relationship with Beloved..."

His lecture went back into the usual drone then, going over concepts I had already grasped. I had read *Beloved* back in high school, to broaden my horizons, and I had been gripped by both all the horror going on and the exhausted, traumatized but still proud Sethe. Meanwhile, the guy, who had ignored an entire key paragraph of text in his eagerness to challenge Sabine, had probably read nothing beyond comic books.

Sabine was smart. She stood up for herself. She had a strong sense for people's bullshit and would call angry men three times her size on theirs. She recorded everything she could get away with, and she'd use people's attacks on her against them by going public with them.

I can't help but admire her...a little. Even if I was sitting here plotting to manipulate her and ruin her enthusiasm for staying at Markinswell.

I had tasked Nathaniel with finding out as much as possible about Sabine's background and family. I knew she was poor and here on a full scholarship. Nathaniel theorized Sabine's claims that this was her best academic opportunity were less than accurate. Rather, Markinswell represented her only full-ride scholarship and her only financially viable way of going to college.

I watched her typing away on her laptop as the lecture went on. If that were true, we really could ruin an impoverished girl's one chance of making it in mainstream journalism. All on some principle I didn't entirely agree with. I didn't want those concerned with the mixing of the student body to lose their voices, but their vindictiveness about the whole thing left me feeling soiled.

But here I was, coming up with the plan and acting on it,

because that was what was expected of me. The leader of the Alpha Omega Gentlemen's Club either solved the campus problems brought to him, or he lost his position.

I followed Sabine at a distance as she walked to the journalism survey. I loved watching her walk. The sway of her hips in her professional-looking broomstick skirt. The determined set of her shoulders. That she never wandered or seemed uncertain.

I was sure that most of her confident demeanor was just very good acting. None of the shit she was going through could be comfortable for her. Inside, she must be frightened as hell by some of the things happening. Some of it unsettled even me. And, to be truthful, made me angry. I'd like to find the ones sending the rape threats and deal with them myself. People like that were not men. They were he-apes who needed some time in a cage or just a good beating. They did not help the cause of returning the campus to its former state one bit. And fear of rape was the weapon of the weakest sort of male.

I suppressed a surge of desire, watching her toss her hair unconsciously as she stepped through the door of the classroom. If only we weren't at odds, I would have pursued her for real. But school politics had done this, not I. And if it took putting her through some drama to embarrass the school for its decision, I had no problem doing that.

Now, however, I needed to focus on step two of my little game, making contact. I was certain I could dazzle her if given the opportunity.

I sat two seats away from her in class, casually staying in the corner of her vision, turned just a little in her direction, so she could see my face. Perhaps even notice my increasing, curious glances and my smile.

So, what sort of man is your type, Sabine?
Friendly?

Reserved?

Commanding?

Charming?

She couldn't like an aggressive approach amid all this chaos. I doubted I could befriend her without her becoming very wary of me. She must know at least something about campus politics by now. *If I showed myself as ethical, would it prove me as trustworthy in her eyes?* Any great lover knew that trustworthiness, or at least a good pretense of it, was a great way to get past a woman's guard.

I caught her sneaking a peek at me and glanced her way almost unconsciously, warmed by the touch of her soft, soulful gaze. Everything else about her said she was a seasoned professional, too good for freshman year, too good for the people harassing her. But those doe eyes of hers drew my gaze magnetically, making my breath catch. The challenge of dealing with a woman who had some natural power to go along with her intellect intrigued me.

I grabbed a swallow from my water bottle. When I straightened, I saw one student behind her reach for her hair. I caught his eye and shot him a warning glare. The kid, a skinny freshman with glaringly red hair, blinked at me and sat back in his seat. *That's better. Enough of this acting like we're in third grade.*

Sabine seemed oblivious, until out of nowhere, she spoke up, "So, are you going to introduce yourself, or are you just here to keep the freshman boys in line?" She didn't even glance up from her copy of Michael Herr's *Dispatches*, but she was smiling faintly.

"I was planning to introduce myself, before the fool seated behind you tried his hand at pigtail-pulling." I kept my voice gentle and amused, very casual. There was no reason to be tense, even if that soft gaze left me just a little off-balance when she turned it back to me.

"Well, all right, then," she teased gently. "So, what's your name?"

"Blake. Blake Morrison," I replied smoothly and offered my hand.

She shook it. Her skin was soft, her grip firm. "I guess you already know who I am."

"Yes, well, you're difficult to miss." I chuckled softly and noted how quickly she took her hand back. "You seem a bit surprised by my approaching you."

"Well, it's refreshing to run into men on campus not threatened by having a woman around." The corner of her mouth quirked.

I scoffed gently. "It takes a lot more than having a woman around to make me feel threatened. Besides, you're much easier to look at than these fools. Look at them." I gestured around in mock-annoyance, though really, many of my associates could have used the attention of an excellent tailor.

She snorted. "I didn't think Dr. David Morrison's son would have a sense of humor," she confided as the rest of the class filed in.

I maintained my smile, but just barely. She had already started researching some key players around campus, including me, apparently. *This is going to be tougher than I thought.*

"I get it from my mother," I countered without even blinking, and she laughed a little. "I wasn't aware you had heard of my father."

"Well, he owns most of fraternity row, so the name gets bounced around on campus now and again." She was teasing me. Testing me. Seeing if I was just friendly or just trouble.

I shrugged. "We've little in common besides the name." Dad was far older than Mom, an old-guard conservative with courtly manners and a predatory business sense. I was less concerned with tradition and far more with making my mark on my own terms. "He would have a far bigger problem with your being here than I ever could."

She lifted an eyebrow. "So, what side does that put you on? He owns your fraternity house."

The challenge annoyed me a little. "Yes, he owns the building. But not its occupants. Especially not me." I kept my smile on.

"Good. I like a guy who can think for himself." Her eyes twinkled as she turned away when the professor walked in.

Meanwhile, I was suddenly dealing with a happy little catch in my chest. I caught my smile widening and schooled it back down to something more placid, a little concerned. I couldn't tell why she affected me so much, but she did. And that was dangerous.

I'm really going to watch it with this one, I thought as I settled in to listen to the opening lecture.

CHAPTER 5

SABINE

THE SECOND BLAKE started circling my periphery, I felt it. Not just because he was one of the most famous seniors on campus, but because I remembered him. Personally. It had taken me a while to put a name to a face, but once I had, I had been on high alert for his return.

He had been at the protest that had scared Mom the first day I had moved in to the dorms. He hadn't held a sign; he hadn't shouted; he had hung back, aloof in his black leather jacket, dark hair swept back, amusement quirking his Cupid's-bow lips.

He had done nothing to impede or intimidate us. In fact, he had laughed at the one guy who had. If I hadn't known better, I would have assumed he was a student journalist covering the protest. He had been just that, detached.

He was also sexy as hell, something I hadn't been able to appreciate under the circumstances. In that sea of angry faces, his calm interest had stood out, but so had his looks. He was big and sleek, muscular with a deep voice and air of authority I found just as compelling as his intense gray eyes. When he had spoken to me, I had felt my toes curl as his deep, purring tones caressed my ears.

I had still kept my head. But our brief conversation stuck in my mind all day and most of the night. Just like the curve of his sexy smile. And that was a problem.

Every talented journalist did her background research. After taking photos of almost thirty of the guys regularly giving me problems and doing image searches on them, I had compiled folders on each one of them. What I had learned reminded me of a recent sociological study done on abusive, sexist male gamers; they were the closest thing this campus had to underachievers.

Most were here because of rich parents or other connections. None had successfully arrived on academic merit, scholarships, or achievement-based grants. Few if any had extracurricular activities or had anything besides "single" set on their Facebook profiles. They had academic and code of conduct warnings. They had social issues. Some had criminal records for public outbursts, harassment, or stalking. Having rich parents had smoothed the road for them considerably.

Something about Blake's presence at the protest had reminded me of another similarity between many of my antagonists. Of the thirty-one guys I had files on, twenty-three had pledged Alpha Omega in the last three years. Twelve were members. The lowest-ranked, lowest-performing members, all first-year, most probationary or on notice.

I almost wanted to slip back into the school's files online to see if I had missed anything, but I had taken too much of a risk doing that the first time. I didn't particularly care about the ethics of it—an excellent journalist took certain risks—but if they caught me in this case, they would expel me. That could end my career. No way was I letting that happen.

The link between poor performance, insecurity, and hating

women was right there for anyone with the right background reading to see plainly. I could probably write one hell of an exposé about it. But I felt like my very presence and refusal to back down was stirring people up enough. I'd just start working on a book on the subject, publish it once things simmered down. I also worried I might get sued by an overprotective parent of one of these assholes.

But I had bigger things to worry about than planning a future book as revenge for what I was going through. I walked around with the lid firmly clamped down on my simmering anger, refusing to dwell, studying even harder in response. I was going to crush these guys academically instead of letting their behavior make me falter. Ultimately, aside from on a personal-safety level with some of them, I wasn't worried about any guy on that list.

But Blake Morrison? He worries me.

He and four others ran Alpha Omega. They might not have sent the men protesting against me, but they had ties to them.

I sat back in my chair and stared at my screen, where I had brought up a few photos of him from the campus newspaper. Confident, aloof, his smile just a touch too arrogant, he looked every inch a rich guy's princely son. His beauty had annoyed me at first, before we had spoken. He never seemed to take a terrible picture, have a bad hair day, or miss a chance to look just a bit more well dressed than the surrounding men.

It was subtle dominance-signaling, backed up by his height and powerful build, and that voice that shook me down to my bones. I didn't like dominant men, especially when I didn't know what their real motives were. And most especially when they made me weak in the damn knees. He had so much charisma that I fell for it even as I knew I was doing so, even as I tried to stay objective. Even after understanding that he might be part of the same group of men that wanted me gone—and might be untrustworthy because of it—he had still caught my interest way more than I ever wanted him to know.

He even smelled good. I don't know what his aftershave was, but I doubted my dad ever could have afforded a bottle. Lime and spices, with a note of bay leaf. He had taste in his scents, like in everything else.

Why the hell is he interested in me?

Why did he watch me so long before approaching?

Is he genuinely curious, or is he planning to mess with me?

I hated that I had to think like this about guys. But I wasn't stupid, and I knew how to read a crowd. Aside from a handful, most of my fellow students tolerated me being there.

The stunningly successful, hot-as-hell Alpha of Alphas at Alpha Omega had not just taken an interest in me out of nowhere, even if there was a lack of women immediately around to compare me to. His Royal Hotness wanted something, probably bragging rights about bedding me.

I stared at his photo for a few seconds longer, then realized it was getting late. I had promised Mom to catch up with her before sundown tonight. She was getting less tolerant of night-time calls now that she was alone, saying that it always made her feel lonely afterward.

So, I pushed Blake out of my head and called her.

Mom picked up after one ring. "Hello, dear! Are you eating?"

I had to think about it. She knew me too well. *That's what I forgot to do after class.* When I was on a project, the first thing I started ignoring was sleep. The second was eating. "Uh, the dining hall's still open. I'm going down after I talk to you." I couldn't keep the embarrassment out of my voice. "I just wanted to catch you before dark."

"Good, this house gets too empty with you not here and your aunt out on her new job. And her new boyfriend. When it rains, it pours with that woman. I want her luck." And off she went, straight into gossiping about the family. Alone in my dorm room with the window at my back, I cradled my phone against my ear and felt a sad longing for that chilly mountainside cottage. At least the people back home liked me.

I chuckled cheerfully. "Mama, she's widowed twice over."

"Good for her. They were both assholes. The new one's a baker. He's sweet like sugar himself, going to make her fat and happy. Like I said, I want her luck." Her voice was too bright, I realized, like mine. She wasn't taking my being away well, but there was more to it than that.

"You've been into Grandma's brandy, Mama? Careful with that stuff." I kept my voice teasing while I worried. Mom only drank when upset.

"Only a little," she conceded. "This house is very empty."

I swallowed hard. Sometimes, after wearing myself out dealing with my childish classmates all day, after forcing myself to attend class and study and do everything I needed to while fighting all day for my very right to be there, I thought hard about giving up and going home. But if I did that, I would blow my best chance of making it as a journalist and pulling my family and me out of poverty. "Mama, you want to come visit next weekend? There's a nice place near campus where we can have sandwiches."

"Will those boys ruin it?" she asked warily, and I laughed despite the sudden tightening in my gut.

"I won't let them. Besides, I've made a few friends. One of them is helping me with keeping up my blog." I didn't bring up that Billy was, in part, doing that by helping me sneak a look at things like school files and criminal records. Apparently, the same guys were on his case for other reasons. They didn't seem to need much excuse—being here on scholarship, being a woman, being a guy who was into guys. "You'll like him. He's sweet."

"Dating-material sweet?" She immediately perked up.

I didn't know why, but I immediately thought of Blake.

Blake, who had caught my attention even before he had slid up and turned on the charm.

Blake, who ran a good chance of being anything but nice.

"No, I'm definitely not his type. Besides, I'm trying to focus on my schooling, like you advised me to. Remember?" Mom had definitely had a bit too much of that brandy.

"Still. I wish so many of those boys weren't showing their rotten side so often," she sighed. "It's not good to be alone too long. And I worry that they will make you hate men."

I laughed genuinely then, though there was a nervous edge to it. "No, no, it doesn't make me hate men. There's a specific type around here that's causing problems. The fewer prospects they have, the more they seem to hate me. It's different with those who will work for their success, like Billy."

"Oh well, some men have always been trash. I taught you that long ago." She sighed. "But then there was your father. The only thing he ever did wrong was die young on us."

I swallowed a sudden lump. "Come on, Mama, he wouldn't want you moping like this. I'm doing okay. There are a lot more guys who treat me like just another student than there are acting like we're all nine years old. I'm doing well in class, and I'm adjusting."

"But you're forgetting to eat. Which means you won't be sleeping properly either." She sounded arch again.

I rolled my eyes. "Mama."

"Don't deny it. You can't push yourself so hard without looking after yourself. At least get a proper meal and some sleep. It's Friday night. You can sleep in tomorrow morning." Her tone told me she wasn't listening to any kind of refusal.

I smiled. "I will, Mama. I promise. Just please don't worry so much about me, okay? You didn't raise me to back down from a fight."

"No, I didn't. But I still don't want you getting hurt. And I don't want you too lonely, and I need to know you're taking care of yourself." She was rambling, her voice shaky.

"Okay. I understand. I get it." Maybe it was boring of me to spend my Friday night catching up on things like food and sleep instead of attacking my homework or planning my next blog post. But she was right. I needed both. "It's a little hard to balance everything," I admitted finally.

"Balancing things is a lifelong fight. But if you do not take care of yourself, you will get sick again. I have seen it happen since you were a child, always driving yourself. Take it a little easier. I don't want to have to pull you out for the semester because of pneumonia." I heard her putter around as she slowly calmed down.

"I remember." Through much of high school, in my quest for scholarships, I had driven myself to hospitalization twice. Once from pneumonia, once from exhaustion. I didn't want to go that way again, and I didn't want her to have to worry that I would. "I'll work on doing better, Mama. I promise."

Once I had her off the phone, though, my gaze turned back toward Blake's image, which smiled enigmatically back at me from my computer screen. *What do you want?* I wondered, before texting Billy to see if he had gone down for supper yet.

He hadn't and met me down in the darkening quad, where a thin stream of tired students was still winding toward the dining hall at almost seven at night. "How are you doing?" he asked me at once as I walked up, and we joined the makeshift line. "I heard another guy tried to humiliate you in class."

I scoffed. "Sweetie, he only ended up humiliating himself.

If he wants to sound smarter than me, he has to do the work to know the material better. And guys like that never bother."

He cracked a grin. "Took him to school, huh?"

"I only had to read a paragraph of the text back to him, then the teacher took over and did the rest. The guy was a dumbass."

"Well, you know, the dumber the ass, the bigger the ego." He sounded cheerful, but he was also walking more slowly than I was used to, his hands shoved in his pockets.

"What is it?" I laid a hand on his shoulder and felt him tense under it.

"Alpha Omega isn't accepting any more pledges this year. All the slots went to the guys with connections." He glowered, a mixture of shame and frustration on his face, and I felt my body tense.

"You applied? I didn't know." I didn't know what would make him want to either. I watched him worriedly as he grimaced.

"Yeah, I thought you could use an inside man, after we found out all these guys in Alpha Omega are the ones coming for you so often." He gave me a frustrated smile. "Sounded like a good idea."

"Well, it's the best fraternity on campus, and the one with the most power. But I'm not sure about the company. How much do you know about the guys who run it?" We followed the line inside the bright dining hall, which was as tacky and impersonal as a hospital cafeteria in looks but served excellent food.

"The Gentlemen's Club? Thought we went over them a little. Do you think they're involved with all this? It seems a little low-rent for them." He peered at me as we grabbed our trays.

"I don't know. Guys like that don't keep their positions through petty squabbles over campus policy changes. But a lot of their pledges, who somehow got in ahead of you" —*which pissed me off*— "were at that protest. Including that one creep." I hesitated, wondering how much to tell him about Blake. "Also, one of those Gentlemen's Club guys was there watching."

"Okay, that's a little weird. Did he show that he had a problem with you?" Billy's brown eyes turned to me, filled with worry.

"No. Actually, he tried to chat with me during my ethics seminar." And ever since then, I hadn't been able to get him out of my head. I wasn't used to a successful, confident man turning on the charm with me. "He did the same when we had English together. He gave me a card with his phone number." And I had nearly called it about eight times in the last day. But Billy didn't need to know about my ridiculous, impractical, risky crush.

"Let me tell you what I know about the Gentlemen's Club, okay?" He started piling samples of nearly everything he walked past on his tray: roast beef, fried chicken, potatoes, salad, fruit salad, egg salad, cheese, two rolls, far more than it looked like he could eat. I went for about half as much, and it was still a hearty meal. As we worked on filling up our trays, he talked. "Those five guys have more money and success than men twice their age. They're not quite billionaires yet, but all their fathers are as far as I know, and every one of those guys is well on his way. They've got campus politics on lock. One reason they may have gotten involved in this mess with you is because they didn't see it coming. They're control freaks, Sabine." He hesitated, then added a third slice of pie to his tray. When I blinked slowly at him, he glanced my way. "What?"

"Are you smuggling food to several starving children you've got stashed in your dorm room?" I asked him solemnly.

He snickered and shook his head. "No, I'm just hungry."

"Where do you fit it all?" We found a small table on the

periphery and sat down at it. I scanned my immediate surroundings, wary of the wrong familiar faces. Fortunately, it looked like we had avoided anyone troublesome by coming in late.

"I have a second stomach just for sweets," he declared with a simple grin as he started buttering his first roll.

We tucked in, and I found myself hungry. I gave it a few minutes, downing my sandwich bite by big bite, and then circled our conversation back around to Blake and his crew. "So, what about the Gentlemen's Club?"

He finished cleaning off one of the chicken legs on his plate, chewed, and swallowed. "Besides the money and influence? They're also the guys to beat on the academic honor rolls. The five of them alone have been fighting for the top spots for the last three years."

"So, they're used to running things." And they were brilliant, rich, in control—everything their worst followers weren't.

"Basically. I doubt they see you as a threat, and I don't know why Blake is sniffing around you. I don't trust the guy." He took another bite of his gigantic meal and chewed slowly, staring at me thoughtfully. "I don't think you should either."

I knew he was right. I knew there couldn't be anything innocent about Blake's interest in me.

But once I got back to my dorm room, went through my nightly routine, and crawled into my bed, I started thinking about the hot, tasty, and probably terrible-for-me Blake again.

CHAPTER 6

MARCUS

"BLAKE, IT'S BEEN A WEEK," I pointed out in a teasing voice as we gathered for our supper in the fraternity kitchen. "We've heard almost nothing from your end. How about a report from the front?"

The casual way Blake scoffed as he sat down at the head of the table told me he had run into more resistance than he had expected—possibly more than he had known what to do with.

"Fine," he muttered tonelessly, not making eye contact—and confirming to me that things had not gone as planned.

From the beginning, I had expressed my issues with Blake's crazy plan to seduce Sabine and break her heart so she would leave on her own. You couldn't call yourself ethical and then plot to fuck and dump an innocent woman specifically to drive her away. I understood some guys' reasons for having problems with a co-ed campus, but why did the answer always have to boil down to being vicious to the woman involved?

"Tougher nut to crack than expected, eh?" I lifted the corner of my mouth, and he scowled. "Or did you finally sort out that she doesn't really deserve this?"

"It isn't about what she deserves or not." He ran his hands back through his wavy hair in frustration. "What she deserves is the opportunity she's fighting for. She just needs to be doing it somewhere else."

"So, break her desire to stay here and then come at her with a bribe?" It was a little better than just driving her off, but it was still cold, corrupt, and kind of uncool. *This shit is why I'm not getting into politics after college.* I never wanted to end up in a position like this again, doing something I found patently wrong to satisfy constituents and donors. That was also why I wasn't becoming a criminal defense lawyer after law school. It was the DA's office for me. Dad didn't think I was a fighter because I wouldn't enroll in Officer Training School and join him in the military, but he was wrong. Fighting in court to put away perps and keep more people from being hurt was a much worthier cause than killing one another in some sandbox overseas.

He peered up at me slowly. "I just want her gone, Marcus. Not hurt. But she won't leave any other way. She's too stubborn." And then he chuckled a bit, relaxing, a faint smile drifting onto his face. "Just another thing to like about her, really."

"Interesting." Nathaniel came breezing in with a bottle of green tea, settling his lean body into his chair and eyeing his plateful of chicken cordon bleu. "You've gotten attached?"

"No," Blake answered too quickly, clarifying that he had. "She's just nothing like what Carmody and the others—and that mess with the blog posts—would have led us to believe."

"She's also beautiful," I teased, but the smile dropped off my face when he shot me a bleak look. "No, seriously, what is with that face?" I asked him more gently. "What the fuck happened?"

"I started approaching her in her classes, once in the dining hall at lunch. I began intervening when I saw one pledge breaking protocol to harass her. We had a few conversations. They've started getting longer and friendlier, but she's wary and smart. Also, she's probably the hardest-working person I have ever met in my life. We may have an up-and-coming threat to our dominance of the grade curve." Blake was smiling when he talked about her. It was a wistful smile.

I understood it probably better than he did. *Holy shit, dude. You haven't even fucked her yet, and look at you.*

And then an uncharitable thought popped into my head. *I should let you go on with this—fuck her, fall for her, and end up with your heart broken once she finds out the truth and dumps you on your pompous, overconfident ass. It's what you deserve for going through with this when you know it's wrong.*

"So, what?" I asked. "Now we should go through with this because she's a better grade machine than us?"

Nathaniel chuckled and sipped his tea. "Rubbish. There are no threats, only fellow competitors. If she wants in on the running and has the right stuff, she's welcome. But I'll be beating all of you this year, regardless."

That got a laugh out of both of us, and Blake settled back in his seat. "She just wants her degree and connections for a good internship," he sighed. "She wants to pursue them alone. She doesn't care about our political struggle with the administration. She's focused on her goals, not on causing problems for us men."

"She would be an interesting one to mentor, if half our pledges wouldn't throw a massive tantrum over it." Nathaniel sipped his tea, then tilted his head slightly in concession. "Along with Jude."

I winced slightly, sitting back. Jude was our problem child—just mature and well-connected enough to be part of our quintet, but still way too close to a dumbass teen in both mentality and attitude toward women. Among all of us, he was the one with three hookup apps and an image folder full of nudes. Ironically, he was also the one among us who had the least success with women, though he had a certain boyish charm that disarmed some of them.

"Jude's young," Blake sighed. "He's still too worried about appearance over integrity." He took a swallow of his coffee, which he took black and so strong that you could smell it brewing before you stepped onto the property.

"What's Daniel's take on this so far? Have you talked to him?" Daniel was off "romancing" a sorority girl from NYU who had gone from teasing him online over our school's uproar, to chasing a date with him over the course of three days. He had bragged about it before leaving, promising to return before the next fraternity meeting.

"I think he likes the idea of seducing her, but not much else." A few pledges trailed through, and we went quiet until they followed the second-year leading them up the stairs. I couldn't remember the guy's name. That bothered me. I was usually good at keeping all our members straight in my head, but right now, I was just too distracted.

"Do any of us want to go through with this, besides maybe Jude?" I asked gently.

Blake shook his head. "No, but they have left us with very little choice at this point."

I couldn't agree with his methods, but after a week of this, I knew that behind it all was more pressure than Carmody and those idiots could bring to bear. The Dad Patrol was now on us with the phone calls, asking what we were doing in protest to this "outrageous move by the liberal chancellor and board." My father, the General, had called from Washington, demanding that I find a way to "fix it."

Between the neurotic boys-clubbers on campus and the

old-guard woman-haters keeping the university's funding fat, we were being pushed into this. *I hate it.* "So, you like her, you hate that we're doing this, and you want to go through with it anyway. How is that going?"

"She's wary," Blake replied softly. "Of men on this campus, of Alpha Omegas, of us, of me. She's done her background research on us. She keeps asking me what my interest is in her, and I'm not sure what to tell her."

"Sex?" Nathaniel suggested. "May as well keep it simple and at least half true."

"She's way off from that," Blake admitted after a few seconds' hesitation. "I haven't even touched her yet."

Nathaniel nodded slowly. "Perhaps someone else should try with her. Someone with a warmer approach." His polite smile didn't reach his eyes, and Blake's eyes narrowed in annoyance. Nathaniel could be ridiculously pompous. It was one of his only real flaws.

"I've only managed all of three, five-minute conversations," Blake protested, voice gone sharp.

"I'm not saying to stop trying," Nathaniel soothed in an amused tone. "I say that either Marcus or Daniel should try approaching her. She may find you a bit overwhelming."

That was a kind way of putting it. "I'll do it, Blake. I have an excuse for poking around. You're a frat brother and family, and she's an outsider here."

Blake considered it while we watched him, then grunted and nodded. "All right, then. But if she doesn't show any actual interest in any of us in another week, we must come up with some other way of drawing her in."

"Perhaps we should invite her over," Nathaniel proposed, quirking an eyebrow. "That way, we can all have a look at her, while impressing upon her our lack of sinister motive."

"If the pledges see her here, though..." Blake frowned. "Maybe. We would have to be creative about it."

I let out a laugh, imagining the look on Carmody's face if he saw the five of us seducing her over roast beef and wine. "Creativity is one of my specialties," I declared. "Leave it to me."

Unlike Blake, who had expected to coast into our target's interest with money, good looks, and charisma alone, I was a realist. I knew you had to change your game plan depending on the woman, her preferences, her needs. A lot of guys seemed to view "women" as some kind of monolith, with little difference between individual females. Worse, they assumed women's viewpoints and needs instead of discovering them, which left them even more lost.

Oh well. More failures for them meant more success for guys like me, who had sorted out this simple fact. Brains and empathy were what won over women, not looks or money alone. Hell, Carmody had money, even if he only changed clothes every few days and never seemed to bathe. He just didn't want to be anything but a troll at a computer desk for the rest of his days.

I set out to discover everything I could about Sabine before I even approached her. I had a short timeline to work within, so I pushed myself to get it all done in one night. I started by reading her news and views blog, top to bottom.

I lost two hours to it before looking up and realizing I was already a fan. She was clever, funny, made brilliant points on many topics, even when I didn't one hundred percent agree with her, and didn't lose her cool no matter how abusive the worst men on campus got with her.

"Well, damn." I quickly typed an email to the other Gentlemen with my basic observations:

Sabine's blog is interesting.

She has a well-informed, practical, progressive view, there's nothing inflammatory in her presentation of her political views, and she only becomes controversial when the controversy is brought to her door.

Initially, the intention of her series on the campus was supposed to be positive and optimistic. Apparently, the negative reaction shown in her later posts was exposure of what was being done to her, no more or less.

She's very prolific, with multiple short posts throughout the week and a vlog post every weekend. I've only gotten through about half of what she has online, including looking at her inter-actions in the comments. If you haven't looked at all of this yet, really do so.

Blake was correct. There is a lot more to this woman than we thought.

I ended my email with several thoughts whirling around in my mind.

Was it her presence that bothered me? Or the way other guys were going nuts over it? I doubted it. I didn't really care if some students around were chicks. It was the way the school had shoved it down our throats, the way it was causing some of us to freak out and become disruptive, and how she was caught in the middle of all this that bothered me.

Apparently, it was bothering Blake too. But I suspected, in his case, the feeling was a lot more personal. I was willing to bet Blake was falling for Sabine.

I went back to reading the blog comments. It embarrassed me how nasty so many of my fellow students were being toward her.

How had we gotten so many immature, emotionally compro-mised men among our student body?

She never seemed to lose her cool, no matter how hard it got.

I scrolled through the discussions, amazed by the combina-tion of deep-rooted knowledge and emotional control she showed at every turn. *Is this girl only eighteen?* But some people just grew up faster than others. That was one thing I understood very well. She was no little rich girl with no focus to her life and no real obstacles to push against. Sabine was, for lack of a better word, admirable. And here we were, about to mess with her sweet little head, which was going to be difficult because she was a lot smarter than I thought.

I wanted to drop this bullshit entirely and just ask her out. I liked her. I didn't mind that she was around, and I thought Jude and the younger guys were being ridiculous. Besides, the lack of ethics was making me lose more sleep than I wanted to admit.

It was the first time in a long time my cousin had made a call I had trouble backing. Usually when that happened, it meant that one or the other of us wasn't thinking straight. Last time, it had been me, back when I had thought about harming my girlfriend's abusive ex. This time, he was being irrational. Or rather, he was caving to irrational people to maintain his position. I couldn't respect that. Not in a million years. That wasn't the cousin I had grown up around, confided in, backed up in fights. I didn't know if the power and responsibility had gone to his head, or if he had been operating on worthless information. But it was bad all around, and now we were stuck with the consequences.

There's what I have to do for the fraternity, and there's what I want to do. And I honestly wished they matched up with each other. They usually did, but not this time.

I noticed a donation button at the bottom of her blog page and stared at it for a while before shrugging and setting up an anonymous donation. If we were going to ruin her, I didn't want her to walk away without options for paying for school. I just didn't want her to be broke on top of everything else.

The next day, I went searching for her at mealtimes, as we

didn't have any classes in common. She seemed perpetually busy anyway, only nipping in for a meal an average of twice a day. I wondered when she slept. I wondered when she had time for all the stuff she did. *Did she have a team of friends who were helping her?* The blog didn't mention anyone but her and an "assistant editor," who went unnamed.

I had spent a lot of time going over the information I had gleaned from her blog, and if there was one thing we had in common, it was idealism. She wanted to bring down bad people. Not men, not conservatives, nobody but actual predators and assholes. That sense of justice would make her vulnerable to anyone who could satisfy it.

Blake had a good idea about stepping in when the others were harassing her. It served two purposes. It stopped the ridiculous behavior that only made her angrier and more determined, and it won over a tiny scrap of her trust. I could do that. In fact, it made me feel a little better to do it. So, when I finally caught sight of her bringing a tray to an open table in the dining hall, I started following her and waited for something to happen. After everything, I seriously doubted I would have to wait long. I didn't. As she set down her tray on the small table, I saw a trio of freshmen in hoodies stand up from a nearby table and approach her. They had grim expressions on their faces and their hands shoved deep into their pockets. Their focus on her was predatory.

I rolled my eyes. *Oh, come on, this is getting ridiculous.*

I moved to intercept at once. I didn't care if they were planning to mess with her meal or with her. It was enough. This was not how men should act, and we were men now, not boys.

She saw them coming and tensed, whipping out her phone. The three stopped dead, eyeing one another uncertainly. "You guys want to lodge a protest, go do it with the administration.

You touch me or my belongings, this goes viral, and I'll press charges." Her voice was firm.

Fucking amateur hour. "You boys take your hands out of your fucking pockets and back down," I ordered, stepping up. All four of them gawked at me. Sabine appeared surprised, but the boys were horrified.

I glared at each of the three. "What the fuck do you think you're doing?"

"She doesn't belong here!" whined one of them, a weird, colorless kid with mousy hair, pale skin, gray eyes.

"That is not your call. What's in your pocket, dirtbag? A knife?" I moved closer to him. The other two were already backing away, searching for an opportunity to disappear into the crowd. But the gray kid, I stepped up to. "Were you planning to stab her?" I demanded as I heard Sabine gasp in horror at the prospect.

"No, it's... I—uh, scissors," he started. "Just for her hair!" he added, as if that made things better.

"That would still catch you assault charges, you dumb fuck," I growled as I watched Sabine lay a protective hand over her dark curls. "And for what? All you'd do is make the rest of us look worse and spend the weekend in jail."

He blinked slowly and dully, as if his brain were still processing things on a kindergarten level. "Why do you care what I do to this cun—"

I stepped toward him threateningly, and he bit back the rest of the insult at the last second. "Be careful how you talk about women around me, dumbass. I'm not one of your idiot buddies." I jerked my chin toward where they were retreating. "Follow them. Don't try this juvenile shit again, or I'll report you myself."

Fear flickered in his eyes as I let my genuine disgust for him show in my eyes for a second. I stared into his until he trembled and then, in my most menacing voice, said, "Go."

He went, throwing down the scissors behind him as he went. I studied them disdainfully. Sabine walked over and scooped them up, tucking them into her pocket.

"You okay?" I asked quietly.

"I'm fine," she hissed. I fought down a smile. The fiery side of her personality was coming out, and I liked it. "Who are you?"

"Name's Marcus. I'm Blake's cousin and fraternity brother." I smiled at her and offered a hand, but she was too guarded to take it after what she had been through, staring at it until I lowered it back to my side. "Apparently some of our pledges have been acting up, so I took it upon myself to keep an eye out."

"That's convenient." She stared at me for a long moment, then sat back down.

I went to the opposite chair. "May I?"

She shrugged and pushed it out with her foot. I took it, setting down my briefcase. "You're trying to tell me you're out policing your own, and that's why you stepped in." She sounded dubious. But then again, she was probably drowning in adrenaline from the Attack of the Guerrilla Barbers.

"Didn't my cousin already explain that to you?" I asked her gently. "I thought he mentioned stepping in similarly."

"All he did was complain about how unmanly the guy was. He didn't identify that guy as a pledge. Though I have noticed that my regular circus of harassers is associated with your organization." Her eyes bored into me.

I blinked back at her, taking Blake's warnings about her shrewdness a lot more seriously. "Yes, that's true. Our pledges are angry, and we're trying to deal with the problem."

She folded her arms, peering at me as if she could read the

truth in my face. I smiled back mildly as she considered me. "Look, this is getting a little weird. Did Blake send you?"

"No, I came around on my own. I was curious. Blake said you were tough and smart, but I think even he underestimates you." I observed her face. She was relaxing, her eyes focusing on me more instead of darting warily around the room, but that didn't mean she trusted me.

"Flattery will not distract me," she muttered, poking at her plate of midday pancakes and sliced fruit with a fork. "Please just ask whatever you're going to ask, say whatever you're going to say, and leave me alone, okay?"

"Oh. Okay." I tried not to take it personally. Nearly getting a chunk of your hair cut off had to leave you with your guard up. And this was my first approach. "Is it always the same guys?"

She raised her eyebrows in surprise. The light caught in the depths of her brown eyes and distracted me so much I had to force myself to focus on what she was saying. "Yeah, it always is. Roughly fifty of them, usually violent, antagonistic, and irrational. I've had to deal with a lot of their bullshit, while not knowing what motive is behind it. Besides straight up hating women anyway." She grabbed her glass of orange juice off her tray and downed half of it in one go.

"The bottom line is, students like that have a problem with an administrative decision they think they should have a say in, and they're taking it out on you. But intimidation attempts? Cutting off your lovely hair? They're all cruising for an expulsion." I didn't much care if someone overheard me. My disgust was genuine. "And making us all look bad."

"To whom? You're all rich—you're immune to any hits to your reputations. Nor do you have to worry about anything you do affecting your employment prospects." She stabbed her stack of pancakes with her fork and left it standing there. I got the impression she would rather have been stabbing Scissors Boy.

"Wow. That's a lot of assumptions." Except it wasn't, and the hard stare she turned on me told me I had misstepped. I was the guy from the military family and less wealthy than the other Gentlemen. I did not quite have the immunity that people like Blake did. But as soon as the words left my mouth, I remembered that my "not quite" was being measured up to her "not at all."

"It's a lot of facts. There are fewer than a dozen full-scholarship students at this school, all of us face abuse, and there are no consequences for it. There are very few consequences for anything that non-scholarship students do, from what I have seen." Her voice had switched to all business. I suddenly realized I was in the middle of an interview.

"Look, I'll concede that there are a number of students here from wealthy families, that daddy having a pile of money covers for a lot, and that there is a chunk of the student body that takes advantage of all of that. But not all of us are that kind of..." I trailed off in frustration as I saw the corner of her lovely mouth turn up.

"Not the issue. If this school's culture didn't have problems on a wide scale, I wouldn't be experiencing them on an almost hourly basis." She stared right into my eyes with her deep ones.

I swallowed hard, not because she intimidated me. I appraised her. Warmth rushed through me, heading straight for my cock. Then I realized why Blake had experienced difficulty sealing the deal with Sabine. She wasn't just smart and on the ball. Sabine was amazing and got past my defenses like they were nothing.

"Well, you shouldn't be experiencing any of this," I insisted. She scoffed, but I pressed on. "I mean it. This isn't how you argue for or against reforms at the school. Your presence here isn't some kind of personal slight against us. If it weren't you, it would have been someone else. You were right to tell them to take this to the administration. Their fucked-up handling of this has caused far more disruption than your presence ever would by itself."

"Are you just telling me what I want to hear?" she mused as she withdrew her fork and used the edge to cut off a bite from the pancake stack.

"No."

For maybe half a minute, she was quiet, face thoughtful as she drained her orange juice. "It's weird that the only guys who get that, besides my friends, lead the fraternity whose pledges seem to want me dead."

"Not dead, just gone." But my stomach tightened at the glance she gave me.

"Mikey Carmody doesn't seem to think that would be enough," she challenged.

I winced and nodded slowly. "Mikey Carmody has been a thorn in the fraternity's side since before I joined the student body." I sighed. "I don't have anything good to say about him. He's the oldest guy at the university. His grades are crap compared to the rest of us, and he's doing nothing good for our reputation. Frankly, I think they should ban him from campus."

"But you're not the one dealing with his threats and attempts to disrupt your life. If you're really worried about containing your more sexist members, probably start with him." She sounded tired and angry—nowhere near as together as on her vlog. But then again, if what she was saying was true, she had been under siege almost constantly. That would have worn anyone down.

I saw my opening and jumped at it. "Look. I get that you don't trust us over at Alpha Omega because of Carmody and some other shithead pledges. But with everything going on, I want to make this right, and I know Blake does too."

A sarcastic gleam entered her eyes, and she rested her chin on the heels of her hands. "And how do you plan to do that?"

I gave her a conspiratorial grin. "Funny you should ask that. I was hoping you'd consider coming over to our fraternity house for a late dinner tonight and seeing for yourself."

CHAPTER 7

SABINE

AFTER THE NEAR-ATTACK on my hair and my conversation with the charming but slightly evasive Marcus, I was left feeling pulled in two directions.

On the one hand, I wanted badly to see what these men who led Alpha Omega had to say for themselves, and whether they would do anything about Carmody and their wayward pledges. On the other, it felt as if I was about to walk into a trap.

What should I do?

I couldn't ask Mama for advice—she would tell me to stay far away from that place and let no man on campus get me alone. I could ask Billy for advice, but he would probably tell me I was crazy for going, too. My common sense was on the fence. Staying away from potentially dangerous men—especially when they wanted to get me alone on their turf—was always the most practical answer. But if I didn't go, I wouldn't have the chance to find out what was really going on with their pledges and Carmody.

Maybe I should have a recorder running the entire time.

New York had single-party consent. I could legally record them without their knowing. And I could download a security app in case I had to call for help. It was the beginning of a practical compromise, but I still didn't know if I wanted to go through with it. It sure didn't help that both Blake and Marcus were smoking hot, and Marcus seemed to be reasonable most of the time. I was almost thankful for the obnoxious edge to Blake's ego. It helped me remain objective about him, given his handsome face and tight body.

I got back to my dorm room to discover a note attached to the door. Warily, I removed it and unfolded it. It was nothing more than a warning that the dorm water would be shut off the next morning. Sagging slightly with relief, I fumbled my key into the lock and let myself in.

Everything was where I had left it. I shut the door behind me, locked it, and turned on my light, setting my backpack on my bed. Apparently, they already knew that Carmody was a problem...or was he their scapegoat? They claimed to be trying to do damage control and keeping an eye out for him and the others who were causing problems. Marcus alleged that if I went to this private dinner of theirs, they'd answer all my questions. It could be an invaluable opportunity. Plus, I'd get to see Blake and Marcus again.

I didn't take either of those attractive men's interest in me seriously, but the attention felt nice after over two weeks of taking people's crap. Marcus and Blake also seemed to be the only people on campus besides Billy who could keep up with me on a conversational level.

Funny how so many of New York's best students turned into incoherent troglodytes when anything shook them up.

I just wished I knew what the Gentlemen's Club's agenda was. Sunny, reasonable Marcus seemed more honest and thoughtful, and he didn't have Blake's edge of arrogance. Blake was more toe-curlingly sexy with a voice that could captivate me, even reading from the dullest text. But there was something cold, imperious, and demanding about him.

Blake commanded.

Marcus persuaded.

I did not understand what the other three did.

But I knew that just getting the chance to interview them would give a whole additional dimension to my coverage of the campus backlash.

Maybe I should wear a recording device. But not only did that feel dishonest, I also suspected they would somehow catch me. I would have to get proper rest ahead of time to make sure my mind was sharp enough to either conceal the device well or to retain all the details without help. If I showed up at all. Though, I wanted to. But I had just plowed through an exhausting day, nearly been assaulted, and dealt with the prospect of not one but two hot Alpha Omegas who seemed to have an interest in me that went well beyond their desire to do damage control for their fraternity's reputation. Marcus's eyes had shown a tendency to wander over my face and body like a caress when he wasn't paying attention, or thought I wasn't.

Could I take advantage of that? No. Never in my life had I used my sexuality to manipulate people, and I didn't feel like changing that now. But I definitely wanted to have as much control over the situation as I could. I was walking into enemy territory.

I flopped into my desk chair and booted up my laptop. Something metallic slipped out of my coat pocket and clattered to the floor. I gazed down—and felt a finger of cold run down my back at the sight of the scissors. I slid my hand over my hair, safely tucked away in a prim bun. Those fabric scissors would have chopped a ragged hole in my hair. Maybe the scissors should have been turned in as evidence. I wondered how to cover the altercation on my blog. I would have to include Marcus's stepping in for it to be accurate, but somehow, that made me reluctant to talk about the incident at all.

I finished booting up my laptop, leaving the scissors where they lay on the floor. I refused to let this garbage scare me. But something about attacking my hair felt personal. I kept reaching back and checking my bun to reassure myself it was there. I wanted a hairdo that would be harder to grab—harder to cut. Maybe a touch punk, but still professional-looking. But I was short on cash, even with the expense allowance from my scholarship helping me out.

Emails from home. Mom had written a rambling one after today's trip to see the fall foliage. My old school was already looking for donations, which made me laugh. *Can't get blood from a stone, boys.* I had more hate mail to go through, along with the comment threads attached to many of my videos. Nothing out of the ordinary, until I opened my blog and noticed a donation alert in the upper right-hand corner of the frame. *Oh hey, one of the college kids or locals sent me a few bucks for coffee.* I opened a fresh tab and logged in to the donation site to see what I had received. Then I just sat there for a while, blinking at my screen, certain it was a mistake.

What is going on here?

Someone had plopped $1500 into my donation account sometime between last night and early this morning. I did some digging. It was an anonymous donation. Not a glitch. Not a mistake. I was $1500 richer now than I had been two days ago.

I wanted to yell. Celebrate. There was always the chance that whoever it was would cancel their donation—but the money was as good as in my hands.

Definitely going to go get my hair professionally done before I went to this "meeting" with the boys of Alpha Omega. I needed to sock away as much of that money as possible, but not all. I was going to have a bit of fun first. Just the tiniest bit of personal reward and upping my professional image.

I wanted to look as good—as put-together, as professional —as humanly possible when I showed up at that fraternity house and when I reported on it afterward. My followers needed to see that despite everything going on, the scissors, the drama, the weird, popular guys from Alpha Omega who wouldn't ever be entirely honest about their interest in me, I was doing all right. I knew I would be an absolute mess after I came back from this little dinner meeting of theirs, even if it went well. I was tired. I had a full class load plus everything else, and I would have to be on my toes throughout the encounter.

I checked my watch. I would have just enough time for a proper hair appointment, a nap, and a change of clothes before heading out to the fraternity house at nine. I should tell Mama about the windfall. I should send some back to her to help her through the winter.

I ended up calling her about it as soon as I got back from the hairdresser. I kept checking myself in the mirror as we caught up, running my fingers through my curly hair that was now cut into a short, chic bob.

"So, how do you suddenly have money?" Mom asked.

"It was an anonymous donation. I don't understand who sent it. But at least one person on this campus supports me." It couldn't have been Billy. He didn't have the cash. It could have been a guilty faculty or administration member. Maybe the mother of one of the rat bastards who had attacked me, quietly supporting me behind her family's back. Maybe someone else who had read my story and had the cash to spare. "I do kind of wish I knew who did it."

"Well, can they take it back?" She had that mix of excitement and worry in her voice that she got every time something good happened unexpectedly—as if she didn't quite trust it not to be taken away again.

"No. I already pulled it out and stashed it in my savings account." I smiled as she made approving noises. "I want to send you some of it."

There was a long pause. "Oh, I can't accept any money from you, sweetheart. I'm the one who should send you something."

"Yes, well, my blog finally earned me some money, and I want to share it. I'm transferring five hundred into the family bank account." I put it in the firmest tone I could, but she twittered in protest anyway. "Mama, please let's not get into an argument over it," I cut her off. "I just wanted to let you know what was going on."

"I..." She trailed off, doubtless thinking of all the repairs the house needed, the winter oil delivery, the necessity to stock up on food in case she got snowed in.

"Mama, come on. I'm keeping most of it for myself. I just want you to have something to help this winter since I can't be there." My heart was beating fast, and I felt a sudden surge of apprehension. *Will she be all right up on the mountainside without me?*

"All right," she sighed. "Thank you. It will help. I just don't want you feeling like you must look after me. You're too young to fuss over me. Wait until I am old and can't work for myself."

"I know, Mama," I responded warmly. "But this will give me peace of mind too."

"Well," Another pause. "Get something nice for yourself while you are fussing about me. Then save the rest."

"Oh, I did. I got my hair done. I'll send you a photo." I sounded so excited that it embarrassed me a little. *Yes, it was pretty, and yes, I loved it.* But normally, I didn't spend a lot of money on my appearance. I had too many other, more important things to pay attention to.

Unfortunately, Mom knew this just as well as I did and picked up on it right away. "Your hair? What's the occasion? You don't have a date with one of those boys, do you?"

"Uh—" *Oh boy.* I had just put my foot in it. "Um, I'm interviewing the leaders of the most powerful campus fraternity for my blog," I blurted. "They're wealthy and influential, and I need to look like their equal."

"By having your hair done? Why didn't you buy a suit or something? I want to see this hairdo." She sounded so skeptical that I had to squash a surge of panic.

I sighed and sent her a couple selfies. It took her a few moments on her ancient smartphone, but she finally pulled them up. "It's short, but I love it. My baby looks so grown."

"I can't go in there looking plain and normal. The bun wasn't cutting it." I glanced down at the scissors still lying on my floor and shuddered.

"It's awfully pretty. Are you certain you aren't making yourself prettier for these boys?" The naked worry in her voice made my throat tighten.

I opened my mouth to tell her about the lunatics with the scissors, who tried to drive me away from campus by cutting off part of my hair. But then I realized the panic it would have put her in.

"Mama, I need to look good for my audience. And besides, I will dress to impress." In one of my suits, which I'd had meticulously tailored and which were, unlike the glittering hairdo, strictly business.

"I'm worried. Are you sure this isn't a date?"

With five guys?

I'm not sure I could handle that much attention, even if that's what they had invited me for.

I closed my eyes, lying back against my pillows. Two of the men I was going to see were attractive enough to tempt me into thinking along those lines. But I already knew I had to keep my guard up. These men were obviously after more than just a repair to the school's reputation. They wanted something else from me, and I still wasn't sure what it was.

"I'm sure, Mama. I promise."

CHAPTER 8

SABINE

IT WAS dark and getting chilly by the time I finished my walk across campus to its tiny fraternity row. I didn't enjoy walking in the dark, not with so many hostile people around. But I wasn't about to back down from this meeting, so I hoofed it over there, glad that at least it wasn't cold enough to leave the street coated in black ice.

Alpha Omega House was a sprawling Dutch Revival home, three stories tall, with a gambrel roof and heavy timbers, like an elegant version of homes from Lovecraft's stories. It loomed a bit spookily in the dark; the maples lining its driveway reduced to dormant skeletons after the last windstorm. I caught myself listening for crickets. It seemed like only a month ago I was hearing them constantly out my bedroom window, but the cold had silenced them for the year.

I made my way up the parquet-patterned brick walkway, feeling my stomach jump around inside me as I smoothed my heavy gray wool coat over my thighs. I had my best suit on under it and my single, plain gold necklace and earrings. Conservative makeup—though I hadn't been able to resist dark crimson lips. My whole vibe was a slightly retro, women's power wardrobe, right down to my riding-style boots, which I had meticulously polished before leaving.

Nobody looking at me could tell, just by sight, that I wasn't wealthy and successful myself.

Finally, I stood before the enormous arched door, which looked like something from a medieval castle, and rang the doorbell. "Moment of truth," I sighed, feeling both nervous and excited all over again.

For all of my plans to dress in a power wardrobe and keep things strictly business, I couldn't help but wonder... *Would Blake like what he saw? Would Marcus?*

I would find out soon enough.

When the door opened, I braced myself for an ugly surprise—Carmody, squinting out at me with hate in his dull eyes. Instead, to my shock, Blake himself stood behind that door, a smile on his face that widened slightly as his gaze swept over me.

I swallowed hard as I studied him—all decked out in a sleek black suit, tailored perfectly to his form, tie tack and cuff links in gold. It was simple, subtle, and utterly elegant. He outshone me completely.

"Welcome," he purred in that amazing voice. His gaze skimmed over my new hairdo, and he tilted his head slightly. "You look lovely. Please come in."

I tried to ignore the flush of pleasure I felt at the compliment, but it didn't work.

He stepped aside, and I walked past him into a warm, high-ceilinged hallway with a pocket ceiling and heavily carved wood paneling. The whole thing had an ancient vibe to it, but clean, perfectly repaired, with antique-style electric fixtures. As I assessed the entryway, I noticed the fraternity crest high on the wall facing the door, with two actual suits of armor standing beneath it. I blinked between them, then eyed Blake and lifted an eyebrow. "Very ostentatious." It was beautiful but had the appearance of a museum, if you ignored the rack of boots and sneakers, the coatrack and umbrella stand on either side of the door. I let him take my coat and hang it up, biting my lip at the brief brush of his fingers. "So, is it just going to be you five?"

"Yes," he replied, leading me through the inner doorway into a broad living space with overstuffed couches, a few tables, an entertainment center, and an antique snooker table. "We thought you would prefer that. We barred the pledges and first-years from the fraternity house for the next two hours."

"Oh," I breathed, relaxing a bit more. "I see." That helped a little, even as nervous as I was. But when I realized that I kept staring at him as we walked, my doubts came flooding back. Both of them in one room. And me caught between attraction to the two of them. I just wanted it to go away. If they found out I was interested, they'd use it to toy with me.

Maybe I shouldn't have come.

I am in over my head here.

I felt that for certain the minute he opened the door. But I couldn't run away. Doing it now would make it clear to him that I couldn't handle this. That I couldn't hold my own. And that just would not happen.

"Have you had any further difficulties since Marcus spoke to you?" he asked gently.

"Just the usual hate mail." I didn't go into detail. "But that's daily."

"I see. That's unfortunate. Sadly, when you break new ground—or are used to break new ground—some level of hate is inevitable." I made a noncommittal sound, and he chuckled. "But don't worry. You won't be getting that from me."

"That's good to hear." When I finally followed Blake toward the scent of steak and spices, I almost stopped short, turned, and walked back out. I kept my smile on, my nerves under wraps and my stride even, but my heart started beating so fast it hurt.

It was uncomfortable enough being there with two men whom I didn't quite trust but was attracted to. But as soon as we walked across the polished wooden floor and went through the archway into the grand dining room, I knew I was in even more trouble than expected.

Marcus sat near the far end of the long trestle table that dominated the room. His pale skin shone against the black of his tuxedo. His black hair was slicked back from his widow's peak, and his black eyes danced as he caught sight of me. He raised a hand in a brief wave. I returned it and then glanced around at the other three—who all wore black tuxedoes and, with no exception, were assorted varieties of smoking hot.

Oh shit. I think I may be in trouble here.

There was an empty seat between Marcus and the head of the table where Blake settled. Directly across from the empty seat was a powerfully muscled blond man with pale amber eyes that reminded me of a cat's eyes. His strong Germanic features and fair skin made him appear as if he might have walked out of a sculptor's studio. Now and again, he tugged unconsciously at his tie band, as if unused to the constriction around his muscular neck. As he glared at me, I saw his golden eyes widen just slightly.

Beside him, a tall, lean man with a narrow face and sharp nose regarded me, slim fingers steepled in front of him. He had auburn hair that tumbled in waves to his jawline like the hair of a medieval prince, and his almond-shaped brown eyes had dark red highlights in them, just like his hair. He appeared to consider me more seriously than the others, a thoughtful little frown on his face that seemed deeper and more genuine than the smiles I saw everywhere else.

The last one looked younger than the others and had already ditched his tie and unbuttoned the top buttons on his crisp white shirt. He lounged in his seat almost sullenly, his smile twisted up slightly at one side, more of a smirk than anything else. He had spiky white-blond hair, so pale that his eyebrows were hard to make out, and the darkest blue eyes I had ever seen. He was shorter than the others, but bulkier, as if he tried to make up for his lack of height in the gym. Somehow, he irritated me more at first sight than even Blake had, but I returned his smirk and moved toward the empty seat between Blake and Marcus.

"Gentlemen, this is Sabine, our guest for the evening. As I understand it, she has several questions for us about our organization and the behavior of certain of our pledges. I trust you will give her your full cooperation."

"Yeah, well, she can fucking wait until after I get some food in me." The shorter blond grabbed up his knife and fork and attacked the plate of steak in front of him. His poor attitude snapped me out of my daze. I found myself ironically grateful. It was like a splash of cold water, bringing back my focus.

It was only then that I noticed the source of the smell. They had loaded the plate in front of me—medium steak, grilled to perfection, creamed spinach, and a baked potato with butter and sour cream melting into its split.

Oh boy. That looks like about 10,000 *extra sit-ups.* But I wasn't about to hold back. *How long had it been since I had a delightful meal like this?* I winced slightly. Last year on my birthday, when Mama had taken me to that family restaurant. And I knew at once that whoever was doing the cooking for the fraternity would have sniffed at that tiny, dry steak, thumb-sized spud, and salad bar dominated by iceberg lettuce.

Rich guys. This is probably every day for them.

I shrugged off the youngest one's rudeness as he shoveled

steak into his face, now and again eyeing me from just over Marcus's shoulder. Blake shot him an annoyed glare and cleared his throat, which he ignored. "That's Jude. You must excuse him—he has no manners." And that annoyed Blake.

"Better no manners than no balls," Jude shot back, the smirk deepening. "You're the one inviting Admin's pet female to dinner instead of kicking her off the campus." He eyed me coldly. "Yeah, you heard me, bitch."

Oh shit. So much for a civil meal. My eyebrows rose. "Sorry, what? I don't speak fuckboy."

Marcus burst out laughing. "Jude, get your boxers out of your ass and stop being a dick. The poor woman hasn't even tried her food yet."

"I don't give a fuck," came Jude's sullen reply. "She shouldn't be here, eating our food."

I stared at him, then shrugged. Cut myself a chunk of steak, smirked at him, then stuffed it into my mouth. I chewed and swallowed while he glared at me. "Get up and stop me, then."

He sat back, blinking rapidly, almost dropping his fork, and Marcus laughed again. "Don't mind him. He's just salty because his dick's as short as the rest of him."

The German across the table dropped his face into his hand and laughed silently. Jude shot Marcus a murderous stare and muttered, "That's not what your mom said."

"The one trying not to laugh at our junior associate is Daniel, our resident exchange student. The one with the hair is Nathaniel. He's annoyed because we pried him away from his computer for this."

"I'll manage," Nathaniel shot back with a bored tone. His gaze slid over me, and I suddenly felt self-conscious all over again, though his neutral expression didn't change. "Just as long as this doesn't take all night."

"I brought fifteen questions total, only some of which will

need elaboration," I reassured in my most businesslike tone. "I'll be publishing highlights of the interview online." Which also stood as a warning that if they caused me any problems, I would publish that. Noticing Jude glaring at me continuously, I had to admit, no matter how cute he was, the fact that he was trying to pick a fight with me this early made it clear to me that there would, in fact, be problems.

That's just fine. If he's going to be a dick, I'll just interview the reasonable ones, and he can choke. Meanwhile, I'm not letting him ruin my meal.

"How do we know," Nathaniel blurted in a smooth voice, "that you will not spin the interview to benefit your political agenda?"

My eyebrows rose, and I stared back into those mild, cold eyes. "My 'political agenda' is to report what happens. My positive or negative impression will determine what I report—and that impression is entirely up to you."

He lifted an eyebrow slightly, the tiniest smile tugging at his thin lips. "Is that so?"

"Yeah," Marcus remarked in a teasing tone. "Maybe we should just duct-tape Jude's mouth now."

"Fuck you, man," Jude grumped.

Daniel snorted and evaluated me. "So, we are to assume that you are not entirely in agreement with the administration's handling of this situation?" He had a slight German accent, which somehow made him sound more cultured than the others.

"Well, I looked into it," I revealed. "On the one hand, it's obvious that the president and deans were very ham-handed in their handling of this and didn't do much to address any student concerns. And for the record, I agree that's bad praxis for any administration." I paused, choosing my words carefully. I hated that I had to be diplomatic toward a bunch of men openly opposed to my presence on campus. Deep down, I thought they could take their weird issues with women and stuff them. But I was interviewing, and that required a balanced, professional approach. Except toward Jude, who deserved every ounce of bitch I had in me.

"I only learned about how they'd handled the situation after I had already been here for a week. Had I known, it would have heavily affected both my decision and my approach. But a full-ride scholarship to a prestigious school wasn't exactly something I could afford to pass up. And instead of continuing their grievances with the administration—which made all the pertinent decisions—most men on campus who have a problem with what my presence represents take their frustrations out on me." I kept my voice calm and even, and my manner all business. I was being as diplomatic as possible and squashing a surge of anger. I shouldn't have to go through all this.

Jude scoffed, but Blake shot him a look, and he kept his mouth shut.

"So..." The quiet one, Nathaniel, took a sip of his tea as he regarded me. He swallowed and continued, unhurried and almost serene. "You believe you should not be the focus of the students' ire in this. And yet you are taking advantage of the administration's questionable decision. You say you did not know. But now that you do, why not withdraw?"

I stared at him hard. "You know, that's very easy for someone who has never had to worry about college expenses to suggest." He shifted uncomfortably, and I went on. "I had one shot to go to college. One. Because—and I guess to a poor little rich kid, this is a foreign concept—my family has had trouble even keeping a roof over our heads since my dad died. College costs a whole hell of a lot of money, and nobody else offered me a full ride."

"If you're that poor and are too lazy to fix it, you don't deserve to go to college—" Jude started.

"Shut up!" Another voice had chorused with mine, and I saw Blake glaring at the younger man with genuine anger in his eyes. Marcus, meanwhile, was staring at Jude with disgust.

I blinked. *Whoa. Okay, I wasn't expecting that.*

"Jude, if you cannot keep your immature, bigoted opinions to yourself, you can take your meal in your room." Blake's fist clenched, and I saw it shake. His pale skin had gone even paler than usual.

I watched him, wondering about the strength of his response. He had no real reason to defend me. My crush on him sent a little happiness bubbling through me, but I didn't trust it or him. I had come here for an interview, and instead, I was the one answering all the questions. *What's going on here?*

Jude's eyes widened, and he let out a little laugh. "You're really going to send me to my room?"

"I'm saying that if you disrupt this conversation in such an odious way again, your choices will be to leave until our guest does, or leave for good." Blake didn't back down one inch, even when Jude stood up and smirked at him.

"You wouldn't," Jude teased. But then he blinked, and his smirk crumpled. "You're actually serious."

"As a heart attack. If you talk like Carmody and his associates at my table again, you'll find yourself sent away from it. We need intelligent discourse on this topic, not your childish ignorance." Blake stared at him coldly until Jude, finally catching on to how serious he was, slowly sat back down. Then he turned to me. "Essentially, what you are saying is that you have no choice in this matter if you wish to pursue a career path that doesn't involve burger-flipping." His tone was sympathetic, but his expression was unreadable.

I got a weird feeling in my gut, but I answered, letting only a little of my irritation creep into my voice. "That's what I'm saying. Your boy Jude here may think you can work your way into wealth, but I am certain that none of you has ever worked hard in your lives. My mother put in eighty hours a week cleaning the houses of rich assholes like Jude's mommy and daddy until her health collapsed. You think it made her rich?" I stared at Jude until he glanced away sullenly, his ears going red. "No. We lost our home. Now we live at the ass-end of upstate and hang on by our fingernails. And that's with me working part time too." I studied all of them. "You rich boys would wither and die if you had to work that hard for so little. But we do. And we get nowhere, because people like you hoard all the genuine opportunities for yourself."

Daniel murmured something in German before speaking up. "So, you are without options. Administration is doubtless aware of this. And thus, you must either accept their using you for their own political agenda or lose your opportunity." He didn't sound sympathetic, only thoughtful.

"Well, you can't possibly believe I would want to stay here with all these jackasses around, threatening me and trying to cut off my hair. Way too many of you people act like the kids from *Lord of the Flies* the minute something around here doesn't go your way." I saw Marcus wince slightly when I mentioned my hair.

Blake was nodding, face still unreadable. "Many students are trying to make this place as inhospitable as possible for you so you will leave."

I saw red. My voice intensified, hardened, but I didn't get loud. "Well, they can go fuck themselves. Like I said, without college or equivalent training, there's no leg up out of being poor. And since I have to worry about my mother and myself, I'm sticking things out, no matter how many tantrums some of you rich boys throw about it."

The group was silent for a few seconds. "Someone tried to cut off your hair?" Nathaniel asked finally.

"Yeah, I saw the whole damn thing," Marcus cut in, sounding exasperated. "Not any of our pledges this time, and not Carmody, but definitely three guys with a pair of fabric scissors. Right in the middle of dining hall breakfast."

"It is rather understandable that you would be in a volatile mood after such an event," Daniel mused. Beside him, Nathaniel nodded.

I remembered the surge of terror that had run through me when I had seen three furious boys—one armed—running up on me at once. I had held up my phone and prayed it would scare them away like that creep in the laundry room. But I still wondered what would have happened if Marcus hadn't intervened. "You have no idea."

"This leaves us in an awkward position," Blake sighed. "I don't doubt that you are telling the truth, but several of my companions want you to leave."

"Yeah, fuck off already with your sad stories," Jude muttered. "This is our campus. It's too bad some guys are taking it that far, but if you weren't here where you shouldn't be—"

"That is not your call." Suddenly, the luscious meal in front of me didn't seem appetizing at all. I shot Marcus and Blake an accusing glare. "So, this was your plan? Lead me into a five-on-one ambush so you could browbeat me into leaving?"

Blake's eyes widened slightly, and for a split second, I thought I saw something like panic in them. "No. I offered you dinner and a chance to interview us. This is the direction the conversation has turned."

"You must think I'm stupid to try feeding me a line like that. I'm not buying it." My eyes bored into all of them. Marcus was shifting in his seat uncomfortably, and he couldn't meet my eyes. Daniel's expression was mildly uncomfortable. Nathaniel stared at me with a detached interest, as if examining the behavior of a rat in a maze. Jude glared back at me defiantly.

"Hey, look," Marcus forced out after an awkward silence. "I'm sorry Jude's being a dick. And I'm sorry things took a bad turn. How about we just eat, and you ask your questions?"

Another glance around. Blake was nodding, a warm smile on his face that didn't touch his eyes. Daniel was frowning. Nathaniel kept staring at me with all the warmth of a corpse. I didn't even gaze at Jude. I had already dismissed him as a bastard who hated me. "You have one chance," I declared.

"Very well," Blake granted. "Ask your questions."

Jude scoffed. I ignored him as I mulled over which one to ask first.

Why are you so afraid of women being welcome here?

Why did you really invite me?

Why do the five hottest guys I've ever met have to be such assholes?

Does being rich just make your soul and conscience wither up and die?

"What are you planning to do about your pledges' behavior?" I challenged. "I understand that not all of them are guilty of the harassment or attacks, but way too many are."

"Get used to it, bitch," Jude started, but this time, I heard a thud, and he grunted in surprise. Marcus was glaring at him. He had kicked his associate under the table, I realized.

"We are still trying to figure out the best course of action," Nathaniel spoke up, voice glacially calm. "Though most of us wish for you to leave, having you forced out by poor behavior of our pledges will create a scandal. In addition, Mikey Carmody is unstable. Anything he might do to you will reflect poorly on us."

I stared at Nathaniel's masked expression and wondered if

he was a sociopath. "Yeah, God forbid that your resident woman-hating member strangles me in my dorm room or knifes me to death in a hallway. It might make your precious fraternity look bad."

My dry tone got a nervous snicker from Marcus.

Nathaniel sat back, blinking rapidly with a genuinely startled expression.

I braced myself for more bullshit from Jude, but he was silent, and when I examined him, he looked just as troubled as Blake and Daniel.

My blood was boiling. I kept the same low, intense tone. "Okay, let me put this another way. The next time anyone on this campus attacks or harasses me, I'm getting the police involved. Not campus security, the actual cops. He will go to jail, and I will press charges. What are you going to do to make sure that the asshole who gets arrested and ends up showcased on my blog isn't one of yours?"

"That won't be necessary," Blake insisted. "I will allow no one from this fraternity to harass or harm you after today."

There was genuine anger and conviction in his voice. I almost believed him. The part of me that lit up every time I looked at him was fighting with the rest of me. But I forced myself to focus and nodded. "How do you plan to do that?"

"Don't concern yourself with details." His iron determination sent an unexpected thrill through me. It was protectiveness. *But could I trust it?*

"People will say we're in love," I teased, quoting Hannibal Lecter.

He considered me, his expression almost as cold as Nathaniel's.

"No, they won't," he answered flatly. "Like Nathaniel, I am primarily concerned with my fraternity's reputation."

Shock and pain went through me, startling me with its

intensity. It felt like he had deliberately gotten my hopes up and then dashed them. "I was kidding," I scoffed, clenching my fist under the table. *Prick.*

"You seem displeased with our priorities," Nathaniel commented mildly.

"I don't give a shit about your priorities if you place how you look above my personal safety. Or if your fraternity's reputation suffers because you don't keep woman-hating psychos like Carmody and this jackass here—" I eyed Jude "—on a short enough leash." I braced myself to get up, though my legs felt a little numb.

"Whoa. Come on, now. There's no need to start a war." Marcus looked anxious—but I doubted it was for me. "Obviously, you don't want to be harassed or harmed. Obviously, we care. We're not monsters."

"I don't give a shit what happens to her," Jude laughed then stopped short when Marcus glared at him.

Marcus continued, "Well, one of us is an asshole, but still, we're not monsters. Blake has promised you that nothing is going to happen to you at the hands of anyone from Alpha Omega. I intend to help him keep that promise."

"But you don't have any answers when I ask you how," I replied pointedly. "I think you're blowing smoke up my ass and hoping I'm stupid enough to believe it's a cure." I stared between the two of them, ignoring the rest. Daniel mostly seemed all right, but the other two had been ganging up on me since I had come to the table. I'd had enough of this shit.

"Trust us," Marcus soothed, hands spread. "Carmody and the others have been showing their ass in a big way, but that's going to end. You may still get harassed by some others, but it won't be because of us."

"Trust you?" I stared at him, shaking my head. "How can I? You've made it clear you don't give a shit what happens to me."

I saw something flicker in Marcus's eyes then he sighed. "I need to ask you something before anything else happens. What are you planning to report on this meeting tonight?"

I let out a high laugh. *Unbelievable. So that's why he's been nice.* "The truth."

"I was worried you'd say that," he sighed as Blake harrumphed, irritated, and Daniel appeared taken aback. "I get that Jude's not coming out looking too good."

"You write one word about me, bitch, and I'll sue you," Jude growled.

I laughed at him. "I don't have to name names," I pointed out. "But the behavior of the group is not above reproach. And I'm reporting what you said, how you treated me, and how obvious it was that you're playing some kind of fucked-up head game."

Marcus drew a sharp breath. "Okay, granted, I don't really care if you're happy here or not, because you shouldn't be here. But that doesn't mean we're the bad guys. We've just been honest—"

I stood up. "No. You've been manipulative."

I considered all of them. "Jude here is just a woman-hating dick with a lumberyard on his shoulder. He doesn't care if I end up dead in a ditch, just as long as he gets his precious sausage party of a campus back. But he's also the only one of you being honest at all."

Jude closed his mouth with a small snap, eyes widening in shock.

"Nathaniel mostly stares at me like I'm a fucking lab animal. I honestly wonder if robots socialized him. When he says he doesn't care if I come to harm, I believe him. When he claims to show interest in my situation and motives, I don't. To him, I'm just something interesting to study until I'm driven away from this university."

Nathaniel's eyes widened slightly. Then he shook his head and glanced away.

"Daniel's charming enough, but the only real thing he's doing right is mostly staying quiet. I can't trust a word out of his mouth any more than I can trust it from the rest of you, unless it's Jude showing his ass again." I glowered at Daniel, who seemed to wilt slightly in his seat. "And then there's you two."

Marcus stiffened as I turned to him. "You pretend to be chivalrous and sweet, but you've already shown your damn hand. You don't care what happens to me as long as I don't expose you for what you really are. But guess what? That's my fucking job. You invited me here knowing I would report on the results. You knew I wouldn't pull any punches. But you and Blake were more interested in playing with my head than anything else. You think I can't tell? You think I'm stupid?"

"No," Marcus blurted. "I don't. It's just you're disrupting everything—"

"I'm not disrupting shit. If you fucking infants would stop hassling me, I would just go to class, write blog posts about how pretty the campus is and how my classes are going. It's not my fault that so many guys around here lose their shit when someone without a dick walks into your precious safe space." I picked up my purse.

"And as for you..." I turned and stared into Blake's steel-gray eyes. He was scowling at me. I didn't give a shit. "It is not enough to pretend to be noble while being a scheming, manipulative ass under a thin veneer of decency. You say I'm going to be safe? I don't fucking trust you. I may not know what game you're playing with me, but you're playing one. And I'm done putting up with it."

"Nobody will believe your smear campaign," Blake warned me, and I laughed.

"What smear campaign, asshole?" I turned and walked out,

grabbing my coat and putting it on as I stared through the living room at them. "New York's a one-party consent state. I've been recording this entire conversation and sending updates remotely." I patted my cleavage. My phone was actually in my pocket, but I didn't want to point it out in case one of them came after me. "I get any more shit from you or yours, I'll release the entire conversation. Got it?"

I relished their horrified stares before I walked out, slamming the door behind me.

Don't you cry, I ordered myself while stalking off down the street, heading across campus.

Don't you dare. None of them deserves a single tear.

I didn't know what the hell their game was, but I could tell when I was being played.

I can be pissed off.

I can think about revenge.

But one thing I wouldn't do right now was let those bastards make me cry.

My eyes stung. I hated it.

I gritted my teeth so hard that my jaw hurt as I dashed off into the night with my cheeks dry even as they burned from the cold.

"WELL, THAT WAS AN UNMITIGATED DISASTER," Nathaniel sighed, sipping his tea as we sat on the couch. "Apparently Blake and Marcus both underestimated her powers of observation."

I nodded, my coffee going cold in my hand as the sound of the door slamming echoed in my head. That whole conversation with Sabine, I had wanted to stand up and scream at the others for being assholes for most of the meal. I hadn't enjoyed toying with Sabine's emotions, but I was forced into a bad-cop role to help give Blake and Marcus a chance to play the white knights.

Jude, Blake, and Marcus were still at the table, arguing over who was to blame for the fucking debacle. They didn't seem to understand that we were all to blame. All five of us. *And I hated it.*

I had wanted to run after Sabine and ask her forgiveness. Offer her an escort home. Anything to soften the blow of her sniffing out our game. A game I had never wanted to be a part of. I didn't much care if she now had damning evidence against us. We deserved it. And it was time for us to man up and make sure she never had reason to use it.

"None of this would have happened if you hadn't overdone your acting so badly!" Blake shouted at Jude.

Jude slammed his bottle of beer down on the table, sending flecks of foam spurting up from its neck. "I'm a fucking football player, not an actor, you dick. Do you think I was having fun times parroting the worst shit I've heard from my guys? I wasn't."

Blake calmed down slightly. "Yes, well, I didn't feel great about threatening to send you to your room like a child either, but you were really laying it on thick. I started wondering whether you were acting at all."

Jude stared at him. "Yeah, I laid it on thick. Because you told me to. Just saying that shit out loud made me realize how fucked up it all is. I'm never letting you put me in a position like that again, bro. You want to con her into your bed, you're going to do it without my help from now on."

"Or mine," Nathaniel spoke up. I nodded grimly. I was still too pissed off to speak to Blake.

"I'm not okay with what happened either," Marcus declared in his best lawyer-voice, hands up placatingly. "It's clear that we need an alternate plan, because I can't do that to her again."

"You mean pump and dump her?" Jude tilted his head slightly. "Because, honestly? Same."

Blake's face darkened, but he remained noticeably silent for several seconds. Then he took a deep breath and spoke in a low, intense voice. "The idea was to encourage her into leaving, using interpersonal means that would not gain us a complaint to the administration. If we don't handle it through a broken heart, how do we get her to leave?"

"Maybe we don't," Marcus responded, and I regarded him,

a touch of my anger draining away. "There are alternatives. You just haven't been open to them."

More of the red left Blake's face. "I'm sorry? What is your suggestion, then? Make her fall in love and then persuade her to leave, perhaps with a hefty financial gift so she can pay her way elsewhere?"

"Maybe," Marcus replied, sounding a little defensive. "Or maybe we should think more long term. I mean, shit, you're halfway in love with her already."

Blake's eyes widened. "I am not..."

"Horseshit," Nathaniel rebuked, startling all of us into silence for a moment.

Blake lowered his head slightly, conceding as much as he was going to. "I admit, she's very special. And there's definitely an attraction there. But our task is to make her leave the campus. We can't just ignore that."

"Okay," Marcus sighed. "Show of hands. How many of us give a shit whether there are a few women on campus?"

Not a single hand went up.

"How many of us wish that our pledges would grow up, shut up, and take their grievances to Admin and the donors instead of expecting us to harass her into leaving?"

It took several seconds, but in the end, five hands were in the air.

"How many of us want to sort out some way of either letting her stay or getting her a full ride somewhere else, as long as it doesn't disrupt things on campus?" Marcus asked.

"It's Carmody and those like him who are disrupting things on campus," Nathaniel muttered. "And I'm uncertain that accommodating irrational demands born of bigotry is the way to lead the fraternity. We're dancing to Carmody's tune, whether we want to admit to it."

Blake scowled even deeper, but his eyes were thoughtful.

"You have a point. And I don't like that idea much at all. But we still must get this situation under control."

"Well, what's your definition of 'under control'?" Marcus asked, folding his arms.

"Get the damn pledges to settle down. Get Carmody under control. And as for Sabine..." Blake hesitated. I could see the wheels turning in his head. "I want her in hand. I want to make sure she isn't motivated to make negative reports on us. And I..." He trailed off, deep in thought for a few moments. "It bothered me watching her leave on bad terms."

"Yeah, me too," Jude muttered into the mouth of his beer. He took a pull and swallowed. "What do we do about it?"

"All right, so we know we don't want to drive her out or do anything else that will hurt her." Marcus peered around. Each of us nodded. "But we don't want to look like we're backing down against the administration either."

"No," Blake agreed. "But legal and administrative battles are separate from the whole Sabine issue."

"Until the point where they withdraw her full ride and leave her with nothing," Marcus pointed out.

"That means we need to connect with her and influence her into accepting our help in finding a new school, should that happen," Nathaniel mused. "With the glacial way the wheels of bureaucracy turn on this campus, she may graduate before our efforts show any actual results, but if we want to be fair to her, we need to have a safety net ready for her."

It was odd, talking about this, when not even two weeks ago, we had been plotting her downfall. But I could hardly complain, because now at least I could stomach the conversation without feeling like I was betraying some of my basic principles. I, too, was fascinated with Sabine. I had met her in some of the worst circumstances and was still captivated.

How could I turn around and let a man like Carmody

dictate my response to her, when what he wanted went against my feelings on the matter?

Blake eyed us thoughtfully. "What? We charm the pants off her, make her fall in love, then influence her to accept a soft landing if the school reverses its decision?"

"Or maybe just make her fall in love," I answered, startling myself as much as everyone else. I paused, steadying myself with a breath. "We all agree that we'd like to have her in our beds and that we're not actually comfortable letting her get hurt in this conflict at all, let alone hurting her further. Tonight was a disaster, not because Jude overacted or because Blake discouraged her too quickly or because Nathaniel was... Nathaniel." I watched him. He lifted an eyebrow, and I shrugged. "It was a disaster because our hearts weren't in it to begin with."

"Agreed," Marcus responded. "I feel like shit—and not because of her recording us."

"You feel like shit?" Jude scoffed. "Try acting like a fifteen-year-old edge lord antifeminist for an hour, I dare you."

"I thought you used to talk just like that," Marcus teased lightly, trying to ease the mood with a bit of humor. He was always the diplomat.

"Yeah, at fifteen!" Jude rubbed his face. "I grew out of it. I didn't enjoy going back. Hell, I had to drop a bunch of friends because they never have grown out of it, so that shit I said to her gave me flashbacks."

"I'm not happy with putting her through this either," Nathaniel admitted after a long pause. "It is part of why I largely kept quiet."

I set the mug on its coaster and stared over at the empty foyer. "This whole idea we had of making her leave by breaking her heart may have sounded good over beers before we ever even met her. But now, we have, and can any of us stomach continuing against a real woman with actual feelings whose future is on the line?"

Marcus's shoulders slumped. "Yeah, that sucked. Say what you want about classism, I'd be doing the same damn thing in her shoes."

"I don't want to drive her away," I admitted. "Especially when it will destroy her future prospects. I don't care if this university goes co-ed, frankly, and left to myself, I would convince her to date me and not leave. Or, perhaps, date us." I had been polyamorous my whole dating life, but I didn't want to make assumptions about the others. I assessed them. All the others appeared thoughtful, and Marcus was nodding.

"I'd be down with that, bro, if you were cool with sharing," Jude suggested. "And if she's into it. Poly women aren't super common."

"No," Blake mused. "They aren't. We'll really have to test the waters carefully with her. But I'm getting the impression that most of us at least would be okay with the idea."

"I'm on the fence," Marcus admitted. "I've shared women before, but it's always been casual. Any relationship with Sabine probably won't stay casual."

"I can handle it if you can," Blake blurted, never one to back down from a challenge.

Nathaniel sat back, pressing his lips together. "I'm not the jealous type. Nor am I one for traditional relationships. But Jude is correct. Even if each one of us could win her heart, that might just leave her unhappy because she is unable to decide between us. We have to consider her preferred relationship style before we try to convince her to wander off the beaten path."

"We could just spoil the shit out of her," Marcus pointed out. "That could sweeten the deal a lot."

"I'm sure it would, but it won't be enough by itself." I took a swallow of my drink and sighed. "She's anything but shallow, and I'm certain she can't be bought." I shook my head, chuckling, remembering her roasting us on the way out the door. "Either we offer her something genuine, or she'll sniff it out and leave us in the dust. And we would deserve it."

There were sighs and nods of agreement. I didn't think there was a single man in the room who wasn't physically and emotionally attracted to Sabine.

Blake just stood there, eyes narrowed as he processed what we were saying to him. "Just to clarify our plans. The alternate proposal is that we keep her? Share her? And shelter her from any fallout from this conflict with the administration?"

"Why the hell not?" Marcus brightened at the very prospect that Blake and the rest of us were taking this idea seriously. "Can any of us say we don't want to?"

Nathaniel tilted his head thoughtfully.

"Not I," Blake answered.

I nodded. "I want to."

For the others, sharing a woman in a non-casual way might break new ground, but for me, it was comfortably familiar.

Jude looked worried. "How would we present this to the others so they would accept it? They might just see it as us betraying them for the sake of some pussy."

"If she's with us," Blake intoned, "then she is under our control. The situation, framed correctly, would likely ease the concerns of those like Carmody. If we 'tame' her, we won't allow her to be a threat to our way of life, especially if we're talking about plans to help her move on from here. And no one on campus will dare harass her again if she belongs to us."

I had to bite back a retort. I loved the idea of getting to know our little reporter better, but even if she was both polyamorous and submissive by nature, it felt like Blake was jumping the gun a bit. Maybe he was more eager than he was letting on.

Jude sighed. "That's even assuming we can talk her out of hating our fucking guts after tonight." I could see the guilt in his eyes. He was headstrong, a little sexist, and could be a bit of an ass, but the role he had played tonight had fit like an iron maiden.

"Well, we can try it." Marcus panned his eyes around. "I just don't think it should be Blake or me who approaches her first after this."

Blake protested at once. "I am certain I can get back on her good side. She's already attracted—"

"Not without help, you can't," Nathaniel cut in, voice a little sharp. "Any trust or goodwill you had built with her is gone. We can say the same of Marcus."

"Nathaniel has a point." Marcus's face was a mask of guilt. "I invited her here. It must feel like I drew her into a damn ambush."

"This was our idea, not just yours," I reassured quietly. Though Sabine might not see it that way right now. "We must be careful, especially if we're trying to feel out whether she would date more than one of us at once."

Then I studied the others. "Who should approach her first?" Not Jude, I thought immediately. His overacting had probably pissed her off in ways she wouldn't get over quickly. But I didn't say it out loud. He clearly felt bad enough.

"You," Nathaniel offered.

I gaped at him. The idea delighted me, but as usual, Nathaniel's motives weren't clear. "Well, I will not say no, obviously, but why?"

Nathaniel shrugged. "I am too introverted. Blake, Marcus, and Jude have made poor initial impressions. That leaves you."

"Oh," I remarked, outwardly calm, but my heart pounded. I

examined the others. "If everyone else is all right with it, I'll go."

Jude sighed and nodded. "I need some more time to figure out how to unfuck her view of me anyway." The glare he shot Blake clarified that he was still pissed off.

Marcus peered at me. "Do what you can to repair the situation, all right? I know it won't be easy."

I shrugged and smiled, the wheels already turning in my head. There was the powerful temptation to let the others suffer the consequences of the terrible impression they had made and court Sabine on my own. The Gentlemen and I had shared a few women before, and we had parted with them on good terms. We had kept the drama down and focused on pleasure and had been scrupulously honest about our intentions. But everything up to now had been casual, with nothing at stake emotionally.

But we'd approached Sabine under false pretenses. Even if I cleared the air, she'd always remember what we'd done tonight.

I finally turned to Blake, who seemed frustrated. He had gotten his leadership called into question tonight a lot more than he was used to. That, on top of the dinner situation blowing up in our face, had to sting his pride. But despite his dark expression, he finally shrugged. "Don't screw it up."

I nodded, biting back a sarcastic comment. We had dealt with enough contentiousness for one night.

CHAPTER 10

DANIEL

MY FATHER once told me that romancing women was an art, not a science. If your actions had no passion behind them, if there was no honest emotion beneath your interest, many of them could feel it. Once they sensed you were insincere, they took it as a great insult, and most times, that destroyed your chances with them.

I had joined in with the others in deceiving Sabine, despite my father's warning. And it had turned out exactly as he had predicted. She might not have sorted out exactly what was going on, but she had known we were playing games. That was why she had left. And now, she had a recording full of consequences for us if we crossed her again.

Hours later, I lay in my bed, staring at the ceiling. The sprawling old fraternity house had a variety of bedrooms on its second and third floors. My room was small by Blake's standards, but I could have fit my whole Berlin apartment into it. The ceiling had little plaster decorations on it shaped like swirling vines. My eyes traced them as I made my plans.

I wasn't just courting her. I was going to mend fences and

lay the groundwork for all of us to court her. Not to mention, trying to feel out whether she would be into being in a relationship with all five of us before we proceeded too far.

The next day, after getting Sabine's class schedule from a stiff and resentful-eyed Blake, I sat in on one of her classes, ignoring the lecture as I watched her.

I felt a little like a stalker doing it this way, but since I didn't have her phone number and wasn't sure which dorm room she was in, it was my only way of approaching her.

Besides, I wasn't sure, after last night's theatrics, that it would have been smart just to show up at her door.

I judged Blake and Marcus a little for the time they had spent following Sabine around campus, looking for the perfect opportunity to get her attention. I wanted to look as trustworthy as possible to her, and following her around half the day —especially if she was keeping an eye out for us—was the opposite of trustworthy.

Sabine was as lovely as ever, even dressed down for classes in jeans and a nice sweater. Her bright, dark eyes were full of life and intelligence, even if a little sunken from her unpleasant night. Her skin was so smooth that my fingers flexed as I imagined running them over the curve of her cheek.

She also looked tired and wary, as if she had already been fending off people today. Or maybe she hadn't recovered from the mess last night. I hesitated, wondering if I was approaching her too soon. But the longer I waited, the harder it was going to be to catch her interest.

When the class let out, I watched her leave, then hurried through the milling crowd to catch up with her. "Hey!" I called out as soon as I was near enough. "Sabine!"

She paused and turned—and then turned back again and sped up.

"Wait, please!" I called after her as we exited the classroom, feeling silly but willing to sacrifice a little dignity to have my shot with her.

She turned back, rolling her eyes, arms folded as she stepped out of the stream of students. "What the hell do you want, Daniel?"

Well, at least she remembers my name. Though she might just have memorized it for her little exposé.

"I wanted to apologize." I caught up with her and stopped a few feet away, moving out of people's way. "I know everyone made a terrible impression last night."

Her eyebrow lifted. "Okay, well, that wasn't what I expected. But if you're going to use that admission as window dressing for a load of bullshit, save it. I will not be charmed into trusting any of you 'gentlemen.'"

I winced slightly. I normally relied heavily on charm and wit to catch a lady's attention. But she was too smart, too tired of bullshit, and too well acquainted with what assholes we could be if we wanted to. "Okay, that's fair. Especially after Jude's tirade last night."

"It wasn't just Jude. It was all of you." Her hands slid down to grasp her curved hips, and I felt my mouth go dry. "Each one of you was an ass in your own special way, and I already called you out for it, so don't think I forgot in twelve hours."

"Okay, I understand. Even if I didn't say much negative to you, I still should have stood up against the crap going on. I went along with something I wasn't comfortable with for the sake of keeping the peace with my friends. And you're the one who ended up paying the price." I let my regret show. It was genuine.

She dropped her arms, letting out an exasperated sigh. "If you want me to listen to you at all, you've got some explaining to do about last night. And we're not doing this in the middle of the hallway."

"Where, then? Obviously, you won't wish to go to the fraternity house. What about your dorm room?" I kept my smile brief but as charming as possible.

She scoffed. "No fucking way I'm letting you into my space. Pick somewhere else."

I frowned. That stung a bit. And yet, I could understand her wariness. "Fine, let me take you out to lunch, then, to make up for helping to ruin your meal last night."

She considered me for a few moments, then nodded. "Fine. Make it within walking distance."

There was a nice little bistro a few blocks from the main gate of campus. I brought her there, finding us an intimate little table in the back. She gazed around at the frescoes on the walls, then down at the menu. "I'll have a cheeseburger, curly fries, and some coffee."

"Perhaps a glass of wine?" I suggested, but she shook her head.

"Coffee. Burger. If that isn't high-class enough for you, it's not my problem." She practically glared at me, and I held up my hands, conceding.

"No problem, then." She seemed to have a streak of anger against the wealthy. She was right to be defensive and untrusting. She had to fight for her place here, while in most cases, the rest of us had family buy-in to this school that went back generations. I could have coasted my way through if I had wanted, but I didn't. I worked just as hard as she seemed to. I just didn't have to.

"Two cheeseburgers with curly fries and coffee," I ordered when the waiter came around. "Mine medium well."

"Sure," said the slim man with the pencil mustache. "Would you like an egg on that?"

"Over easy." I hadn't ever had egg offered to me on a

hamburger until I came to New York, and I had never tried it. No time like the present.

"Sure." The waiter turned to Sabine with a smile.

"Make my burger medium, please," she replied. "No onions, and an egg, sunny-side up. Please bring some steak sauce for the table, if you've got it."

"No problem. Just give me a few minutes, and I'll be back with your coffees."

When he left, she turned back to me. "You're very diplomatic."

"I'm trying to make amends," I replied easily. "I know it will be a bit of an uphill battle, but since we have nobody to blame but ourselves for that, I'm game."

Her expression softened just a little. "Well, it's true. I know you guys were playing games, and I know you made asses of yourselves. What I don't understand is why."

I opened my mouth to tell her that Blake had been having us play bad cop to his good so he could get her into bed. It wasn't strictly true, and it would have been a knife in his back. I was pretty annoyed with him, but no. I couldn't.

No more games.

CHAPTER 11

SABINE

LAST NIGHT, an old nightmare had plagued me. Reliving the day Mom and I had realized that we had to leave New York City. I had come home from high school to Mom in tears, telling me we had to move to Hellbender to live on her sister's land. We were being evicted. There was no money for a deposit on a new apartment. There was barely enough money to get us there, over to the ass-end of an upstate county, in a town too tiny to offer jobs and too far away for a commute.

Mom, who had fought for five years to keep our heads above water after losing Dad, had cried so hard, her asthma had flared up and nearly landed us with another hospital bill. She had seen it as her failure, but I had known better, even then. The VA, which had never given Mom the proper benefits after Dad's death, had screwed us. As had her employers, who had worked her to the bone until her health had given out. And lastly, the system, which did nothing for its poor.

In the nightmare, all those details had muddled together, but the horrible, raw feeling of failure and betrayal had gnawed at me just as fiercely. Worse, this time, the landlord had locked us out with the truck keys still sitting on that tiny studio's kitchen table, and he wouldn't let us in to get them. The sense of being hopelessly stranded on top of everything else had made me wake up with tears on my cheeks.

I had nearly taken the day off. But Mom hadn't sacrificed her health to see me wussing out and dodging classes, so off I had gone, only to run into one of the last guys I had expected to see.

I had sworn never to see the "Gentlemen" again, and here I was, letting one of them take me out to lunch. As I lingered over my burger, I considered the big, blond German with his intriguing amber eyes and wished that he weren't part of their group. He was every bit as attractive as the others on a physical level, and he did have a lot of charm. But I knew better than to trust him.

Daniel was at least more willing to answer questions rather than ask them. Maybe he had learned his lesson last night.

"What you're saying to me is that most of last night was an act to get me to leave voluntarily, but you were all so conflicted over the fact that you botched it up?" I lifted an eyebrow as I watched his face. Liars usually glanced upward and to the right.

His eyes didn't leave mine at all. "Think about it. Do you really think the most prestigious fraternity on Long Island would allow an immature ass, such as Jude was pretending to be, into our inner circle? None of us would stand for it."

"But you let Mikey Carmody and some guys like him become pledges."

"Carmody is a perpetual pledge. Because his father is a member and a heavy donor, we cannot turn him away. But he's failed every single attempt to gain membership, every year he has been here, because of his own immaturity, poor attitude, and lack of discipline."

I nodded slowly, but I wanted confirmation. "Jude's fuckery was acting?"

"Mostly. He can be an ass, but that can be said of most nineteen-year-old men." He took an enormous bite of his hamburger. He had ordered it with a fried egg on top, which was bizarre for me, but I had followed suit, and it was actually tasty.

I was still very wary. "You and your people are trying to get me to leave."

"Before we knew your full circumstances and got to know you, yes. I imagine that if you weren't beautiful, we might not have reconsidered so quickly. But you are both lovely and spirited, and well, the only men who truly resent your being around are those who want you but don't have a ghost of a chance with you." He winked.

My eyebrow went up a degree farther this time. "And you think you do?" But inside, my stomach was curdling at the very thought of Carmody lusting after me, yet wanting to drive me away, hurt me, maybe even kill me, instead of doing anything sane or natural to follow through on those feelings. Though, Daniel was right; that vile bastard wouldn't have a chance in hell with me.

In high school, dysfunctional, sexist fuckheads like Carmody got the Neckbeard label. He deserved it. He didn't entirely look like one—his clothes were too expensive, and his manner more whiny than pompous—but he ticked all the other boxes. Guys like that were the kind people tolerated only because you didn't know what kind of violence fetish they were walking around with or how much access to guns they had. Nobody wanted them around, least of all women.

"I'm sure our chances are less after last night, but I don't know anyone among the five of us who wouldn't give it their best try. Especially after learning of why you're fighting so hard to stay here."

Was that sympathy in his tone? Could I trust it?

"I'll be blunt," I replied with an inaudible sigh. "You are lucky I am agreeing to speak with you at all after last night." His smile faded, and I saw guilt in his eyes. "I'm tired. I have a full course load, my blog, my mom, and—thanks to guys like Carmody—my personal safety to worry about. I don't have time or inclination to give any of my remaining energy to guys who are going to dick around and play head games."

"I'm not playing head games," he protested gently. Again, his gaze didn't float. If he was lying, he had a lot of self-control. "In fact, I promise never to lie to you."

I blinked at him. That was a lot to promise, especially since he knew I was a reporter. "Really?"

He crossed himself. "On my honor."

I stared back at him. "We'll see. I need to know some things, and if you want me to keep listening to you, I need some answers."

"If I can answer them, I will gladly do so." That smile again. I hated how it warmed me to look at him. Whereas Blake was always serious and Marcus was playful, Daniel struck me as the guy who could talk his way behind the counter at a bank. *Dangerous.*

"Fine. Let's start with the big one. How much danger am I in from Carmody?" I bit one of my curly fries in half, trying to ignore how the thought of that bastard made my stomach clench.

He sat back in his chair, eyes going thoughtful, then hooded. "He's got no record, and he's never been violent in the years he's been here."

"You mean, he's never been violent toward men." It was an important distinction. There were men who were notoriously cowardly when facing fellow males, but that didn't extend to women. In fact, some hated women so much that they would fly into blind rages whenever rejected, or even spoken to in a manner that was less than deferential.

"No." A note of worry had entered his lightly accented voice. "Not toward men. There was an incident with a female literature professor two years ago,"

I pulled out my phone to take notes. He eyed the device, then went on. "The professor was very married and very uninterested in Carmody, or any other guy on campus. But Carmody seems to have lived on a planet with no women for most of his life, because just as with you, he couldn't handle her presence."

"That's pretty messed up." I swiped in a few notes to add to my files on Carmody. "So, what happened?"

"He fixated on her. At first, it looked like a normal crush. But he's always around the fraternity house, and after a while, we noticed some weird things going on. Like his photoshopping her face over those of porn stars." He licked his lips distastefully and set down his burger.

"He also took all of her classes and tried to get her attention in every one of them. He did it by trying to make himself appear smarter and better-read than his fellow students. He couldn't manage it. Then, he constantly asked questions just to get her attention. He started being passed over in favor of other students so that others would get equal time. He found this unacceptable."

I took a swallow of my coffee and sighed. The food was great, but their coffee tasted like nurses had brewed it on the midnight shift. I dumped cream and sugar into it and motioned for him to go on.

"He started becoming antagonistic in class, even arguing with her over the finer points of the text. He showed up at all her office hours with the same attitude. Then he began following her to her car after classes."

I shook my head slowly as I kept up on note-taking. "He was getting closer and closer to stalking her, is what you're saying. The guy escalates."

"Yes, that is exactly what I am saying. There are reasons Blake immediately promised to keep him away from you. No matter what our feelings are about the administration making the campus co-ed, you don't deserve problems from our resident problem child."

"The man is almost thirty," I sighed, and he winced and nodded.

"He's coddled by his parents. This, I suspect, is part of the reason for his perpetually arrested development, but most of it is him. His choices, his decision to haunt Reddit hate clubs instead of socializing normally, all of it." He forced a bite of his burger, as if nauseated by Carmody but not wanting to let talk of him ruin the meal.

I took a few notes. This time, they weren't for a news report since I couldn't report on him with too many personal details or I would get sued. No, this was in case there was a criminal case. I was gathering evidence. "What happened to the professor?"

"She gave him a strong reprimand for following her around so much, and when he wouldn't stop, she took it to the dean. They ordered him to stay away from her outside of class and to submit all his questions via email instead. I'm uncertain whether he continued harassing her over email after that, but I know he started a petition to have all female professors removed from campus as a 'distraction.'" He winced when he saw my face.

"Christ, what an immature ass. Looks like he didn't succeed." I rubbed my temple and took another swallow of coffee, praying the caffeine would kick in soon.

"No, in fact, she still works here. However, this gives you some idea of his usual pattern. He is persistent, obnoxious, tries to enlist others to his side, and cannot stand women who show no inclination to—" He hesitated, glancing around, and I immediately got the gist.

I held up a hand. "I get it. Unless a woman is interested in his baby carrot, he doesn't want us around."

"Yes. He's a *schwein,* for certain. One reason he's never made it past pledge in our organization. But he still keeps knocking on our door and camping out in our common room."

"And you haven't banned him because of nepotism. Because his daddy gives the fraternity too much money and, thus, has too much say in what you do." I couldn't keep a touch of disdain out of my voice.

"That's correct." He didn't sound angry or even annoyed. "Do I think he will make things as difficult as he can for you? Yes, but you have recourse even if we should somehow not be able to protect you from him."

"Are you sure he won't become violent if he doesn't succeed?" I stared at him over the rim of my coffee cup.

He shrugged in response. "As I mentioned, he's shown no evidence of that. Also, I doubt that a man in his poor health could do that much damage."

Unless he got his hands on a gun. But if he had access to a firearm, he probably would have threatened the professor with it. I nodded slowly, then went back to my meal as I thought of my next question. Carmody was the worst kind of man—the kind who was both childish and demanded adulation, the kind who hated women openly and virulently but still expected us to jump on his unwashed cock.

"Okay," I muttered after a bite of burger. "Okay."

"Questions?" he asked with a soft smile.

"I have a million of them," I admitted, and he laughed.

"Well, I'm not going anywhere."

Daniel made an impression. A big one. On my way back to my dorm room, all I could think of was him.

He had promised never to lie to me. He had explained a lot of things. Blake and Marcus were basically exactly as they had been with me in person. Jude had been entirely acting. Apparently, he was young and immature, but still successful and far friendlier than he had seemed. Nathaniel was always that aloof. He was also scrupulously honest. And Daniel? He had worked hard to be a gentleman and purge some of the bad blood between us. And he had never come off that badly during the disastrous dinner.

Belly full of a good burger and curly fries, and with inadequate sleep under my belt, all I wanted to do when I reached my dorm room was crash for a nice long nap. I had earned it.

Once I was in my purple pajamas, all I could do was lie there, staring at the ceiling.

Can I trust Daniel?

Can I trust any of them, or is all of this just another head game in disguise?

Giving them another chance after last night was a tall order. But if what Daniel had said was true, there was a lot more to these guys than the front of militant conservative rich boys that they all wore. And every one of them was interested in me.

Sexually interested.

Five guys. Holy crap, what would I even do with them all?

I had never had a real lover in my life. Just two goofy high school flirtations. Kissing, groping, nothing serious. Now, I had five guys who had somehow gone from wanting me to leave to wanting to fuck me. And when I thought about that, my mouth went dry but not from fear.

I hated being a virgin. Not just because it was awkward to

be one well past the age when so many of my friends no longer were, but because I didn't even know enough about romance and sex to make a clearheaded decision. But the idea of being with them sexually made me squeeze my knees together as lust pressed against my womanhood.

And I still didn't know what to do about the "gentlemen" situation.

Dating one guy seriously, going to bed with him, that was unfamiliar territory by itself. But five? It was pretty damned intimidating. I wasn't sure I could choose between them, aside from Jude, whose shitty first impression had still left me with a foul taste in my mouth, even if it was just an act.

And really, after last night, can I even trust these guys?

I'll sleep on it.

I rolled over and turned off the light. Outside my window, a few flakes of snow fluttered past, and I sighed, pulling my comforter up to my nose.

CHAPTER 12

JUDE

I WAS JUST STARTING to get over my guilt for having treated pretty, clever Sabine so poorly when bad news crossed my desktop.

It had been a rough few days. I had slept little. During that time, Daniel had successfully talked to Sabine and apparently convinced her we weren't such bad, hateful fucks. I just hoped it really had worked. But the anger in her big brown eyes still haunted me.

How was I going to explain to her that I wasn't that guy—or at least, wasn't that guy anymore?

How was I going to clarify that I had been acting and had been uncomfortable the whole time?

I was glad Daniel had stepped in to explain some of it, but I still regretted every damn word that had come out of my mouth that night.

It brought out parts of myself I thought I had left behind. Parts I had put to bed after getting into high school. Parts I was not proud of.

After Mom had taken Dad for so much in their divorce, Dad had spent his partial custody bitching to me about women. He called it "warning me," so I wouldn't do something stupid like falling in love.

"Women are only good for pussy," he would splutter at me, drunk as usual and bitter as hell. "You can hire a cook. You can hire a cleaner. You can even hire someone to bear you a kid. Pussy, Jude. Find yourself a hot sugar baby and trade her in for a younger model every few years. Don't even bother with that marriage shit." I always felt torn when he said that. Now, looking back, I realized he had been a hot mess of a man who had been caught cheating by his wife too many times and had gotten what he had deserved. Back then, though, I had worshiped him.

So, from ten years old to fifteen, I had stayed on Team Girls-are-icky way too long, and way too vehemently. While my friends had fallen in love and experimented with sex, I had pranked the girls in school, said nasty things, talked back to female teachers, and frustrated the hell out of Mom. Dad had poisoned me with his own bitterness, and it had taken becoming my own man for me to purge myself of it.

Time had passed. Dad had a nearly fatal car accident while driving drunk. He dried out and got his shit together. His drunken rants against women had stopped. Then the big dumbass had shocked me by getting remarried and had even started admitting that he had been wrong. The new wife—age thirty—had helped him get his head out of his ass just by being nothing like Mom or all the stereotypes he had been telling me that all women embodied. My stepmother was big-hearted, sweet, patient. A kindergarten teacher.

It was then, just after becoming a freshman in high school, that I had realized my dad's habit of talking out of his ass, and I'd cleaned up my act.

I took a long swallow of my energy drink and tried to wake up. Now, there was Carmody, ten years older than me and worse than Dad ever was. And he'd gone from being a nuisance to being a genuine problem. And the worst part was that other guys, dumbass freshmen, who couldn't think critically yet, were backing him up.

I glanced at the window. Cold dawn light spilled in around my blackout shades. *Fucking insomnia.* I hadn't slept well since going full teenage sexist asshole on Sabine. Not really a surprise, but it still frustrated me. *I needed to focus.* We had a big problem that I had just learned about, and the only way I was going to bring that across to the others was with a clear head.

I had set aside video games for a while, and I was checking my email and feeds when I caught sight of some files forwarded by one pledge. They turned out to be group chat logs between the pledges and some first-years, with Carmody as the most frequent poster.

I thought you should look at this, the pledge's note to me said.

And after reading through all the files, I knew he was right.

Carmody had been talking behind our backs, stirring up the pledges. Every new guy trying to make his place in the fraternity, everyone on our waiting list, was included in the secret chat. I went to the site and checked myself. I had known he was bitching to some of them—he'd never shut up even when we told him to—but I hadn't known it was this bad, that he was reaching out to so many, or that so many were listening to him. And I sure as hell hadn't known he was trying to do all of this without the Gentlemen knowing.

Goddamn it, Carmody, you stupid son of a bitch.

He was acting up again, and this time, he seemed ready to

foment a full-fledged rebellion. It didn't just piss me off. It worried me. *The guys are going to have to see this.*

Unfortunately, it would have to wait for breakfast. I couldn't just shake everyone out of bed at six in the morning because I couldn't sleep.

I read through it again, having to convince myself that it was real. I didn't know what kind of crazy Carmody was, but whatever his problem was besides just plain hating women, it was becoming our problem too.

I printed out the transcripts and started marking the pertinent bits with a highlighter. It was mostly Carmody's statements that were the problem, but he was stirring up some other guys too. I did not understand why the same guys who hung out with me in high school would start listening to a spluttering, aging creep who wasn't even a real member of the frat, but there was a lot about this situation I didn't understand.

I skimmed through each page, marking a few sentences here, a paragraphs-long rant there. By the end, my back teeth hurt and the corner of my eye kept twitching. I couldn't understand how this guy could hate Sabine this goddamn much when she was so smart, spirited, hot, and simply amazing. Except maybe that was the problem. She was all that, and Carmody didn't have a chance with her. And he was one of those pricks who thought the world owed him a hot girlfriend and that any attractive woman who wouldn't fall into his arms was insulting him. So, in Carmody's eyes, she had to go down like the professor he wouldn't leave alone.

I had met guys like that before, though I thought I had left them all behind in high school. Guys unpopular with women, who started hating them and then harassing them and causing them problems. Most of them would have had some success with a bath, a shave, and a few manners, but none of them wanted to make the effort. They just wanted life to be like porn: endless, no-commitment, high-end pussy without their having to do a damn thing to impress a woman or even make her comfortable around them. And when that didn't manifest, they got salty as hell.

If women weren't jumping on their dicks on demand, they were the enemy. No middle ground. No way of fixing it. No taking responsibility for their crusty-cumsock level of hygiene or their massive personality flaws. Women were to blame for the lack of sex in their lives, because women were bitches and deserved to be punished. As did men successful with them. Men like us. And that was the biggest problem. I had read the chats, expecting all his flipping out about Sabine. What I hadn't expected was him being openly against the five of us. He was planning a mutiny.

That fucking turncoat.

I clenched my fists when I read Carmody's words:

They had her over for dinner, guys. Dinner! Black tie and all!

I don't know what they think they're doing. They told us to trust them and not get in the way, but bringing her into our frat house and feeding her steak is not taking care of the problem. They said they wanted the bitch gone too, but this happens!

I think she's just controlling them with her pussy.

Carmody could have written the book on toxic hate rhetoric, and the shit he was saying as he tried to stir up his fellow pledges against us reflected that. At one point, he used the word "femoid." I would have laughed if I hadn't wanted to punch him so fucking bad.

The world had been a better place before bottom-of-the-barrel dudes decided that hating women made up a political movement. *Jesus Christ.*

Maybe I should have expected this. I spent the most time with the first-years. I hung out with the pledges. The only one who expended anywhere near as much energy on our youngest members and wannabes was Marcus. And yeah, some of that crowd had ideas that the other Gentlemen didn't totally agree with—like getting rid of Sabine. But we still took their wishes into account.

So why was Carmody doing his best to turn everyone against us?

My eyes narrowed on his words:

The Gentlemen need to be removed. We need new leadership.

"What, like you? You can't even qualify as a member, no matter how many years you try. And they wrote the rules before we were born, you fuck," I growled as I kept highlighting the most dangerous-sounding bits of his argument.

It was true. Carmody either couldn't or wouldn't adhere to requirements well enough to get in. Whether it was his chronic lateness, his missing pledge meetings, his botching any test we set for him, he came in dead last or close to it every time. Worse than that was his constant, stubborn demand that every pledging requirement be justified to him. He would argue against common-sense rules, like not filling up the common room with vape clouds or trying to take over the entertainment center when a bunch of us were watching something.

Last year, when I had joined, the dumb bastard had almost made it in. All he would have had to do was take his loyalty oath to the fraternity and he would have had his own room here and status as a first-year. But while the rest of us had sworn in, Carmody had disrupted everything by demanding to know why the oath was even necessary. Blake had given him an ulti-matum: swear the oath, or don't get in. Carmody had thrown a fit and stomped out. Another year failed.

Maybe that was why he hated us so much. If it wasn't

Sabine, it would be something else. *Goddamn it, I wasn't this much of a spoiled, contrary fuck even back when I was fifteen.*

Fortunately, I had already been forced to deal with one maladjusted man-child a generation older than me. It was why I knew to watch Carmody more closely than the others. And now, James the pledge, who had only been deferred because he had gone out for surgery unexpectedly during rush, had made sure I knew just how bad it had gotten.

Too bad I couldn't get the others to see it that way.

"This just sounds like Carmody's usual drivel," Blake concluded, tossing the sheaf of papers onto the table beside his empty breakfast plate. "I don't see what's especially troubling about it."

I rolled my eyes. "Blake, I know you're not a morning person, but think. The fucker was up all night reaching out to every pledge on our waiting list, both our deferrals, and every single first-year that got in. Trying to turn them against us. Not just Sabine, us. The guy's trying to, well, I guess he's trying for a coup."

Nathaniel laughed, startling the shit out of me. "That buffoon couldn't take over even if the charter allowed for it. Besides, I doubt that very many of them listened."

"Enough are listening that it's a problem," I replied. His smirk faded, and he lifted an eyebrow, but I couldn't tell if he was annoyed with me or genuinely considering the problem. The dude was like a fucking Vulcan.

"The fucker found out about the dinner with Sabine somehow and came up with this paranoid-ass story about her controlling us. And now he's spitting it out at anyone he thinks will listen."

"All the more reason for us to take control of her," Daniel mused. "It will impress them if we influence her into praising the campus instead of constantly reporting on her harassment. If we have her in hand."

"Yeah, I'm still down with the plan if she's into it—that's not the problem here," I sighed, poking at my eggs. I had barely eaten. "The problem is, Carmody is escalating, and even if he doesn't have the power to mess with our positions, he can still cause all kinds of problems. Especially for Sabine."

Marcus glanced up sharply at that. He had been digging into his stack of sausage patties like he was a grease addict who hadn't had a fix in days, but now he set down his fork. "Shouldn't we just lurk on those chat forums and watch what he's planning, so we can head them off?"

I shook my head. "No, because they won't be doing all their planning online. We've got to confront him in front of the other guys and make them at least understand that he's way out of line and not serving Alpha Omega's interests."

Blake was staring at me, the little frown on his face telling me he thought I was out of line to be taking all this shit so seriously. But I didn't know how else to take it. The alarm bells were ringing in my head just as loud as back when Dad had gone out drinking and I had known he would drive home drunk.

"Fine," Blake agreed. "Confront Carmody in front of the others if you feel it is necessary."

I stared back at him, then puffed out my cheeks, exasperated as I evaluated my fellow Gentlemen. "Can I get some backup, then?"

Nathaniel shrugged, back to eating. Daniel was frowning but said nothing. Blake wasn't interested.

"I'll go," Marcus agreed, breaking the tense silence between us. "Even if it turns out to be nothing, I always love taking a piece out of that prick."

I relaxed slightly. It wasn't exactly a vote of confidence, but I would take it.

The picket lines around Sabine's dorm building had thinned more as the weather had gotten colder and midterms had drawn near. It seemed like most guys had lost their taste for the argument against her being on campus, probably because she wasn't exactly disruptive. If they had all minded their own business, she would have done the same. But Carmody was going to be there and, in the chat logs, had pressured the others into joining—or rejoining—him. This would be an excellent opportunity to see who exactly had listened to his rant. We couldn't just knock them off the waiting list, but I could make sure they were on notice that Carmody was not a guy to be listening to over us.

"I don't get why Blake isn't taking this seriously," I sighed as we walked toward the dorm. "I mean, the evidence is all there in black and white."

"Well, you know Blake. The guy is convinced he can handle anything Carmody throws at us right off the bat. He thinks he doesn't have to be proactive. Your gut may tell you differently, but he only listens to his own gut." Marcus shoved his hands farther into his pockets, his breath puffing white. It wasn't even October 1 yet, and early mornings had still been down near freezing for almost a week.

I wasn't surprised that Blake's own cousin was so open in his criticism. Marcus was usually diplomatic, but there was a tension between him and Blake that had always lingered. Marcus wanted reforms. Blake wanted to stick to tradition. But tradition and Carmody's daddy were the reasons we hadn't been able to get rid of Carmody yet, and just look where that was getting us.

"I just hope his ego doesn't end up coming back to bite us,"

I muttered. "Have you run into Sabine since Daniel talked to her?"

He smiled. "Nah, haven't been lucky enough, and I wanted to give her more of a cool-off period before I started visiting her classes again. I felt like shit after that dinner."

"Yeah, me too." We reached the top of the hill, and I saw the small crowd gathered at the entrance to the dorm building. Only three guys had signs. The rest were just hanging out. But I could already see a fat, trench-coated figure soapboxing to them as they stood there.

How does that prick ever get anyone to listen to him? He had no charisma that I had ever seen. All he had was a big ego, a loud voice, and persistence. "You think he's giving out free bags of weed to every guy who shows up?"

"That would make more sense than them just listening to him," Marcus mused. "But I think he's just saying shit out loud that some guys have been thinking. You notice how most of them are freshmen?"

"Yeah," I sighed. I wasn't too far grown out of my asshole days, and if I hadn't been ahead of the curve, I wouldn't be part of the inner circle. Many eighteen- to nineteen-year-old dudes were still maladjusted edge lords, and some were worse. "Guess he's just appealing to his maturity level."

"Yep." I already knew Marcus wasn't including me in that group. He was normally my closest friend among the five, and he knew what I was about.

When we got closer, I started hearing Carmody yelling hoarsely above the chatter of the small crowd. "We can't rely on the administration to protect our interests. We can't rely on fraternity leadership to protect our interests. She has to go, and if we want her gone, we have to act for ourselves!"

Nobody cheered or even yelled agreement, which reassured me a little. Some guys just kept talking, like they hadn't even noticed his yelling.

"What are you suggesting we do, kill the poor girl?" Marcus called out, sounding darkly amused.

Carmody glanced up, his eyes going blank and his expression of righteous fury fading to uncertainty. And he answered, trying to play off as if he hadn't just been stirring up people against us. "We keep the pressure on until she runs," he insisted.

"What do you mean 'we'?" I wanted to run up and punch him in his fat, ugly face, but I was sure the whiny fuck would press charges. "You're down to five people out here. And you're sure as fuck not telling any full-member Alpha Omegas what to do. You're barely a fucking pledge."

"Just because most of my supporters couldn't make it," he started, and Marcus laughed.

"Your supporters?" Marcus mocked. "Nobody's here supporting you, buddy. The only thing you've got in common with these guys is that you don't want a woman on campus." I studied the guys' dubious faces. "In fact, I'm not sure you even have that."

"Yeah, asshole, and you've already been told that we're handling it," I added.

"Handling what, her tits?" Carmody retorted. All eyes turned to us as the crowd went quiet. "You've been taking her into the frat house to fuck her, haven't you? You'll let her get away with anything for a little pussy!"

I felt rage well up inside me like a rising column of lava. *Stop fucking talking about her like that.* "She's not getting away with shit besides studying for midterms, you dumbass. And you've got who's controlling whom completely backward."

His brow slowly furrowed in confusion. "What?"

"If you see her with us, and you think she's the one calling the shots, you're out of your damn mind." I walked toward him, the small crowd parting for me. I clenched my fist at my side, and I stopped out of punching range so I wouldn't be tempted.

"You say that—" he started.

"I'm saying it too," Marcus said at my elbow. "Go look at her blog. You might have noticed that she's fucking settled down. It helps that none of you idiots have gone after her with scissors in days, but the point is, she's no longer posting shit that damages the school's reputation."

"That's not good enough," Carmody spat. "You want us to stand back and let you deal with her, but then you're not dealing with her. Explain to us why she's still here?"

"We have explained this to you twice, you fucking dunce," I sighed. A chuckle rippled through the group.

Carmody's eyes rolled frantically to take in his fading supporters. "Don't listen to them. They're in bed with her. They don't care what happens to us or this school as long as they're getting laid."

"That is bullshit!" Marcus's anger shocked me a little. "None of us have touched her." But all of us wanted to. Not that either of us was going to bring that up.

"Man, that dinner wasn't even my idea," I added. "I spent half of it arguing with her. Called her a bitch like five times. She was pissed." And I felt terrible about it now, but I wasn't about to admit that either.

Some guys looked mollified. Some, impressed. But Carmody's face turned tomato red. "You're just saying that to make me look bad."

"Carmody, you do that shit just fine all on your own." I sighed. "We're here because you're hassling the other pledges so much, they can't focus on their studies. There have been complaints. From them. About you. Something about sticking them all on a mailing list and spamming them all night with your crap?"

It was only half bullshit. As for Carmody, he blinked slowly, appearing embarrassed.

"I have freedom of speech," he started, but Marcus just laughed at him.

"Freedom of speech saves you from government censorship, not from other people's opinions of how shitty you're being," Marcus reminded him. "And it doesn't save you from any other consequences either."

"Yeah." I glared Carmody right in the eyes until he glanced away. *It won't save you from catching these hands either, you prick.*

"Thanks for coming along," I remarked to Marcus as we walked away. "I don't think he's going to budge on any of this."

"Yeah, well, he can picket in a snowstorm in a couple months and catch pneumonia. Besides, you were still right in having us come down here. Even if he won't listen, some others did." He patted me briefly on the back.

"I guess that's something. At least we weakened his influence over some guys who have been following him." I would have to monitor that damned discussion group after this and see if our intervention had any kind of effect on people's responses to Carmody. "The question is, what do we do now?"

"Seduce Sabine after midterms," Marcus suggested. "Honestly, I believe that the best way of preventing her from disrupting everyone else's lives is to not disrupt hers."

"Some guys are distracted just by her presence," I muttered. Though, that wasn't necessarily a bad thing.

"Well, yeah, but I kind of like that kind of distraction," he teased me.

"Oh, hell yeah. Me too. But I'm not a fucking woman-hater

like Carmody." Or at least, I wasn't anymore. "I just hope I haven't ruined my shot."

"After Daniel's damage control, I'm guessing that depends on how you treat her now," Marcus responded.

I guess it didn't matter who'd come up with the stupid idea to trick Sabine. Daniel had our backs. *But what happens if I can't win her back and just have to watch the others share her?* The idea fucking hurt. But I had gone along with Blake's plan, even when my gut had told me not to. *If I was paying for it now, I had only myself to blame.*

Guess I'd have to cross that bridge when I came to it. If I hadn't burned it already.

MIDTERMS WERE LOOMING, and I was on track to get good grades—if I could stop being distracted by thoughts of the Gentlemen. All five of them seemed to have an interest in me—but all five had also deceived and antagonized me in the past, and I didn't know whether I could fully trust what Daniel had told me. And even though I had every reason to be pissed as hell at all of them, that wasn't what I felt when I thought of them. Not even when I thought of that hot asshole Jude.

As much as I knew that he deserved to have me tell him to go fuck himself, I just couldn't bring myself to consider it anymore. Yell at him, sure, but not shoo him off entirely. Trusting him after that, however, was another matter entirely. Even if he had been putting on an act when he had been so damn insulting, I didn't know whether I could trust someone who could invoke that kind of behavior in himself. It was one reason I had never dated any drama students. Once you knew they could pretend to be someone else so fluently, how could you trust them to be genuine?

But still, I needed to push Jude and all the rest of them out of my head and focus. Midterms. Four papers, one project, five standard exams, all in the next two and a half weeks. I had started prewriting for some papers, but every time I tried to get another few paragraphs out, I stared out the window instead. Thinking of them. Again.

Blake's intensity, softening with affection.

Marcus's humor and wit, tempered by warmth.

Daniel's charm, improved by sincerity.

Nathaniel's strange, detached brilliance, warmed by desire.

Jude's smoking-hot body, made more attractive by his figuring out when to keep his damn mouth shut.

I couldn't decide which, on that primal sexual level that made my thighs rub together when I stopped to think about it.

I liked Marcus the most. I was most impressed by Blake. Daniel knew how to make me blush with a bit of gentle teasing. Nathaniel's air of mystery only made me want to know more about him. And Jude, well, I wanted to see just who he was behind that virtuoso asshole performance. Not to mention that I couldn't get the way Jude moved out of my head.

Dating five guys...at the same time.

What the hell am I thinking, contemplating that kinky unconventional romantic scenario?

Deciding between them didn't just feel natural. I didn't want to choose. *Was I poly? Or was I just greedy?*

I needed to get my head back into school, not my lustful longing. It didn't help that it was so damn cold. I had thought I'd left behind the worst of the cold when I had moved out of the Catskills. But when I observed the scene outside, I could see frost forming on the lawn, leaving it glistening in a way that promised slippery-ass ice in the morning. I would have to keep to the salted walkways.

I sighed and rolled onto my back, staring at the ceiling. Mostly what I wanted right now was for people to stop demonstrating outside my dorm, to stop pestering me in class, to stop leaving nasty notes taped to my door. Blake had promised to keep people off me and he had, at least some, for the problem had lessened considerably. But it wasn't gone.

Still, I had held off on publishing about that disastrous dinner, about Daniel's approaching me after that, and about the Gentlemen's involvement in this complete mess. The jury was still out on what they were planning for me, and I wanted more facts before I published anything.

I hadn't even updated my vlog since that dinner. My readers would wonder what the hell was going on with me. But when I thought about what to say, I drew a blank. If I wasn't talking about the Gentlemen, what did that leave me? The fall colors couldn't be enjoyed properly in this cold, or with pick-eters and pranksters to worry about. I wasn't past midterms yet, so I couldn't report on them.

I checked my watch. *Damn.* I had gotten into the habit of taking a two-hour nap after supper if I had nothing going on, just to refresh my brain, but the cold outside and my general exhaustion had stretched it to three. Ten p.m.—too late to call Mama. I tried Billy instead.

"Hey, sweetie," he said into the phone. "How's my favorite reporter?"

"Fucking tired. How are you doing?" He sounded entirely too smug. I wasn't surprised. At last check-in two days ago, he was on his third date with a fellow freshman. Fast work. I almost wanted to tell him about the five guys who were appar-ently interested in me—but the very thought made the words catch in my throat.

He'd warned me about them. About the fraternity. About dating anyone at this school. If I told him, or my mom, and then things got bad, I'd never live it down with them.

"Well, David is still wonderful. He took me out to dinner yesterday!" Billy sounded so excited that I cracked a smile.

"Good. He'd better keep treating you right, or I'll have to come over and kick his ass." I was only half kidding. Billy was still one of my anchors in this crazy place. And he was a decent soul who deserved to be happy.

"Oh, don't you worry. If he does, you can get in line behind me. I'm not letting any more guys play with my heart." He laughed and then sobered almost at once. "How about you? How are you holding up? I noticed you haven't updated in days."

"Yeah, it's mostly just needing to study. That, and it being cold this early in the year, is sapping all my energy." I stifled a genuine yawn. "I conked out for three hours after coming back from the dining hall."

"Oh, I get it. Are you still being bothered by a bunch of jerks and perverts?" His voice had gone hushed, as if it worried him that someone might overhear.

"Some. I mean, that dick Mikey Carmody is still yelling outside my dorm building every damn morning and evening, but the crowd that comes to watch is under ten people now, and most of them do nothing." I couldn't tell how much of that was the Gentlemen's interference, how much was discouragement from the cold, and how much was guys realizing that the world hadn't ended just because a woman was attending classes with them.

I really freaking hoped for that third one. Because all this craziness over one person was kind of ridiculous, on top of the stress it had caused me.

"Maybe some of them have come to their senses," Billy mused hopefully. "That would be refreshing."

"Yeah, it would be. I don't think the one guy is ever going to stop, though. He seems to be getting worse." And that scared me way more than I wanted to admit to Billy. It was the same reason that my mom knew very little about this situation. I didn't want her to lose sleep just because I had to.

"He hasn't done anything violent to you?" Billy sounded fretful suddenly, and my heart sank. I hated ruining his mood.

"Man, if he had, it would be all over the net by now. I don't mess around, you know that. Besides, I already gave the warning to his fraternity leaders that I was calling the cops on the next one of their boys who messed with me, and that includes pledges." I sounded more confident on the phone than I felt.

"I wonder if they did something." Billy sounded a little distracted. "I hope they're smart enough not to want that kind of trouble."

"That's a nice thought. I'm not sure about those guys. They're a little hard to read. But they seemed to take me seriously, and nobody's run up on me or left notes on my door since they promised to step in." I didn't know if it was because of my threat or because of their interest in me. But it was still a somewhat hopeful sign.

Isn't it?

"That Carmody guy, though, he's never going to stop until he sees real consequences. Maybe not even then. He may need to be locked up." The thought of it made me ill. In a perfect world, his smelly, woman-hating ass would already be in jail for harassment. Instead, I had to wait until he literally tried to hurt me, break into my dorm, or otherwise make good on his threats before the cops would do a thing.

"Too bad you can't just sic a lawyer on him. Maybe get a protection order?" I heard him drum his fingers thoughtfully.

"If we end up sharing any classes, that will become difficult to enforce." I sighed wistfully. "Maybe I could keep him the hell away from my dorm or anyplace outside of class. Not sure how it works."

"Well, I know you've got some spectacular research skills, so why not put them to use?" He sounded even more distracted.

"You know what, that's a good idea. I'll do that while I'm figuring out what to put in my update." I didn't know how that would reflect on Alpha Omega or the Gentlemen, though. I considered contacting Blake about it.

Wait, why does he get a say in what I do to protect myself from a pledge he's so far failed to rein in? He's lucky if I tell him about it at all.

"Okay, sweetie. Well, the boyfriend's texting me, so I'd better get back to him. You going to be okay?" His voice was soft and apologetic.

"No problem," I replied cheerily. "You have a good night, okay?"

A wave of loneliness hit after I signed off. Normally, I was too busy to be lonely. I could have distracted myself with studying or working on a video or blog entry, but I thought more and more about the possibility of getting a protection order against Carmody. That way, I wouldn't have to wait until he harmed me before I got the police involved. All I had to do was wait until he violated the protection order. But that might affect more people than just him.

I resented having to run this by the Gentlemen before I went through with it. They didn't deserve to have that much input in my decisions. But I didn't want anyone caught up in the problem who wasn't directly involved.

I'd warn them. That's it. I wouldn't ask permission. Not even from Blake. Even if his commanding voice and manner made me weak in the knees, he still didn't call the shots in my day-to-day life. I did.

I checked the law online. The protection order could be conditional. It could prevent Carmody from approaching me within a set number of feet. That would allow us both to walk around campus or even take classes together without his being allowed to confront me. Not that he seemed to enjoy doing that without a crowd at his back. I wondered if he would even say anything in person if he were alone.

I called Blake. He picked up almost at once.

"Hello, Sabine. I didn't expect to hear from you this late." He didn't sound annoyed, only curious. "Is something wrong?"

I forced myself not to apologize for bothering him. "Fewer things are wrong than usual, but I still need to tell you what's going on. It's about Carmody."

I heard him suck in air. Now, he sounded annoyed. "What did he do this time? I heard he was still demonstrating outside your dormitory."

"That's part of it. But I'm more worried about him escalating, as he did with that professor. He's losing supporters. His crowd is smaller every time I walk out, but he just seems more furious." I felt a little silly trying to explain my concerns. "I really want to deal with him—"

"I told you we would handle him," he reminded impatiently.

"Except you're not handling him," I cut in. "He's still there, he's just as crazy, he's escalating even as he loses support, and I'm honestly dreading what he's going to do next. I haven't even been online in a few days because of the shit he's been sending me."

"Block him and move on. I'll handle him personally," he repeated.

"No," I responded flatly.

"No?" He sounded genuinely offended.

"No. You may have gotten through to some others, but

Carmody is crazy, and if you have been talking to him, he isn't listening. And you were already plotting to drive me out, remember? That's not a good way of getting anyone to trust you. It's presumptuous as hell to just expect me to take you at your word. How good is your word, really?"

"Better than you think, apparently. So, if you're not relying on me to handle him, what do you plan to do?"

"I'm looking into getting a limited protection order." *I should have said I am getting a protection order. I hate how I soften around him.*

"Though that is possible, his parents are wealthy and over-protective, which means they'll come armed with a lawyer. You might be in for a protracted fight." He went quiet for a few seconds, and I heard the tapping of computer keys. "But if you insist on going through with it, my family has a lawyer. I could retain him for you."

My jaw dropped. "Oh wow." *Why was he doing this? Out of interest? To minimize fallout? Or because he wanted me to rely on him and his protection, no matter what I did?*

"I'll do it on one condition," he offered in a businesslike tone. "I want you to report the whole truth when you do so, especially once Carmody violates the protection order and goes to jail. I want it known that we aided you in protecting yourself."

"I have no problem giving you due credit," I pointed out a little breathlessly. I wasn't used to anyone running to my rescue —financially, legally, or otherwise. The only one who cared enough to was Mama, and she just didn't have the money most of the time. "I keep telling you I intend to be objective."

"Good." He hesitated a moment, then questioned in a tender voice, "How are you doing?"

I swallowed hard, feeling a flush of warmth go through me

at the question. "I'm fine. Gearing up for midterms." I took a deep breath. "It's been hard to study with all these distractions." I meant Carmody and his pals, but they weren't actually the biggest distraction in my life right now. Instead, the big distraction was on the phone with me. Blake and his four companions.

I didn't know why, but I hadn't realized just how attracted I was to them until Daniel had come to me with his apology. If I hadn't been drawn to them, all I would have felt on learning they were playing mind games with me would have been outrage and the desire for revenge. But that wasn't all I had felt. I had been hurt. Disappointed. And suddenly very aware of my loneliness and frustrated desires.

They hadn't been just assholes. They had been attractive, charismatic assholes that I still wanted to impress, even after walking home in a rage from dealing with their bullshit. And when Daniel had then caught up with me later, apologized, and explained the situation, I had felt a little better about what happened. I was still processing the idea that they were all interested in me and apparently, somehow, weren't jealous of one another.

"I see," Blake mused. "If need be, I can send you a tutor. I feel partly responsible for your current distraction."

I opened my mouth to tell him no, that it was fine. That I didn't blame him because he and the others were now haunting my dreams at night. The sexual dreams that made me wake up with damp panties, tingling skin, and disappointment that it hadn't been real. All that came out of my mouth instead was, "Oh?"

"Yes. I feel I need to apologize personally. I know Daniel ran some interference and explained the situation to you, but I feel responsible for what happened."

That was a change, a welcome one, but it gave me

whiplash. It was like he had dropped the "trust me just on my word, for I am flawless" act for something more honest.

"How so?" I didn't know if that dinner and its emotional push-pull had been his idea or someone else's, but if he wanted to wear the bull's-eye, I wouldn't complain. I had found it telling that the guy who had approached me to apologize first had been the one who needed to the least.

"I signed off on that course of action," he revealed. "I did it without a full understanding of you, what you are going through, or what the consequences would be."

Okay, yeah, that's progress.

Blake's arrogance was his least attractive feature, and his setting it aside to any degree was promising. I bit down lightly on my lip, my heart beating faster. "Why did you do it?"

"Because we were under tremendous pressure to rid the campus of you. Not just from Carmody, but from several other pledges, first-years, and donors." He paused, letting that sink in.

I sighed. "Your parents."

"Yes." His tone stayed flat. "There was a financial and social gun to our heads, and we capitulated without full possession of the facts."

"What changed?" I couldn't tell if it was the journalist or the woman in me that was more curious.

"You." He cleared his throat. "It has become clear you are not the problem here. You represent the problem."

"What is the problem, aside from women being on the campus?" This was, again, different from what I had expected from him.

"The problem is the administration's refusal to listen to our concerns or even to provide us with a forum to air them." I heard rustling and creaking as if he were shifting in his seat. "You are here because you saw an opportunity to go to college. If you were not here, they would replace you with another woman in the same basic position. It's very clear that our administration has exploited your desperate circumstances to turn you into a political pawn, and that is entirely on them."

"I see." *That's part of what I have been trying to tell you. But there is no point in bringing that up again now.* "Is there anything else?"

"Yes." Another pause. He seemed to weigh every word especially carefully. "Going through that farce of a dinner made me realize that we were all wrong. That not only did your presence disrupt very little, but that we—I—do not want you to leave."

My mouth went dry. "Oh." But then I frowned. "But what about your donors? Your parents?"

"We have wealth of our own. And it's time to cut the cord. If my father or Carmody's parents or others withdraw support, we will step into the gap. Whatever the case, the administration should not punish you for their mistakes."

I let out a shivery breath. "Thank you."

"I would like the opportunity to make it up to you. Not by helping you protect yourself from Carmody, but by assisting in your studies. And by replacing the meal that I helped to ruin."

The tiny hesitation in his voice intrigued me. "Are you asking me out on a date?" I challenged—fairly gently, but a challenge, nonetheless.

"Yes."

I huffed out my breath, thinking of Billy's warnings, Mom's fears, my own misgivings. After last time, I didn't know what he might have up his sleeve. But I was still curious. I still wanted him, despite my best judgment.

Take the bait? Even knowing that it may be bait, and I may end up disappointed, hurt, and angry again?

"Find us a good steak place, and I'm in."

CHAPTER 14

NATHANIEL

MY MIND WAS full of extraneous things as I took my walk across campus to Sabine's dormitory. The taste of my breakfast. Marcus and Daniel's low-key argument over who would ask Sabine out after Blake's turn with her. The three species of birds I had observed in the bright-leaved trees on the way over. The song I had caught from a passing student's cranked-up headphones.

I had an eidetic memory, and sometimes it was a nuisance. Distracting. Disorienting. It stuffed my mind full of facts and sensory information that became difficult to sort through at times. Yet it was also useful in both my schooling and certain aspects of my day-to-day life.

Mom had called me her "little professor" until I had outgrown the "little" part. Although I had intended from the start to go into the sciences and not academics, I could still understand why. I had practically grown up in tweed and had been prone to giving lectures. I supposed it was a mild case of intellectual narcissism, but I tried not to be obnoxious about it.

But given all the missteps we had made with Sabine,

someone had to be the brains of this operation, and Blake's pride and the demands of his position ruled him out. Besides, brains were exactly what Sabine needed right now. They had sent me to provide academic support, and that was exactly what I was going to do. There was no one among us who was better for the job.

I paused at the corner across from her dormitory and checked my phone for the list of her classes I had obtained, as well as the schedule of her tests. She had five midterm exams and a variety of projects. The projects, which were mostly in journalism, I could not help her with. But getting high test scores—and helping others to do so—was a personal specialty of mine.

"Introductory journalism. Panel on journalistic ethics. Survey of journalism and publishing law in thirty countries. English literature. Introduction to political science. Calculus. Astrophysics." I lifted an eyebrow. Eighteen units. It was quite a heavy course load for a first-year freshman. Especially taxing given the environment they had forced her to study in. But she seemed to hold herself to a superior standard, so I wasn't all that surprised.

There was still a small, milling crowd gathered at the main entrance to her dormitory building. I could see Carmody in their midst, trying to stir them up. His face was red. His eyes were wild, and despite the cold, his visible skin was coated with sweat. His appearance was like a mad prophet plucked from a street in the Holy Land, left unbathed and unshaven for a week, and squeezed into a trench coat.

"If we let them get away with this, if we let that female stay in our space, it will open the door to dozens of them. Another men's space taken over by females who refuse to know their place in the world!"

"You mean on my dick?" a blond freshman crowed, and his buddies laughed.

"This is serious!" Carmody's voice cracked with emotion as he went a shade darker.

I gave the scene a quick assessment and nodded once. I could understand Sabine's concerns about this individual and why she wanted to get a protection order. The more boys who surrounded him, joked about the situation, or lost interest and walked away, the wilder he got. I still remembered how he had blindly risked expulsion in his rage because a female professor wouldn't sleep with him. Everyone else remembered too.

In her shoes, I would probably want a protection order myself.

Yet part of me wondered if Sabine doing so wouldn't goad him further. Carmody had an "I do what I want" streak far wider and deeper than I had ever seen in an adult human being. It was like he had stopped maturing in his midteens. I didn't know if trauma, spoiling parents, or the internet had made him like this, but he was rapidly becoming a danger to himself and others. *Especially to Sabine. And that, I cannot abide.*

I turned and walked down the street, losing myself in the thin crowd before turning and circling back behind the building. I did not want to set Carmody off or give him any clue what I was doing. He had already spied on us once and gone into a fit over that awful dinner party. No point in clueing him in that I was visiting Sabine. People would definitely talk, and not just Carmody either.

The parking lot was dotted with patches of black ice. I skirted around them and around the little half-melted and refrozen snowdrifts that had dropped on us late last week. I had absolutely no idea why the weather resembled that of early January, but here we were, seeing our breaths every morning as we stumbled off to class. And this was just a foretaste of what we were in for. *I hate winter.* But winter would come, regardless, and there was no point in distracting myself with that either. I needed to focus on Sabine and how I could be of help to her.

Blake rarely asked me for anything outside of my usual duties to the fraternity. But we needed to regain Sabine's trust and goodwill, and that would require work. Gifts of help. And I was more than a game, especially since I wanted the chance to speak with her alone.

The others talked about "sharing" her like some delicious sexual treat. I was nowhere near that immature. I wanted to know her mind. I wanted intellectual intimacy, the sharing of ideas. I wanted debate and negotiation. I wanted to impress her. There was something offensive about her thinking of me as a cold-blooded insect of a man. But perhaps I deserved that assessment. I'd given her nothing else to go on.

At least I wasn't as bad off as Jude. I'd forgotten how insufferable he had been at that age. We had gone to high school together. He was two years behind me, a close acquaintance then if not a friend, and I had been the one who had sponsored his pledge to Alpha Omega. The others had demanded to know why, and I had explained his potential and how much I had seen him mature in the three years of knowing him.

His behavior the night of that horrible dinner had practically given me flashbacks. He had truly been intolerable in his midteens. But he had grown. We both had. I wanted to show Sabine that I was not as she expected.

As for Jude, well, he would have to prove who he really was to her himself. It wasn't entirely fair, given that his bad-cop act had been Blake's idea. But he had gone along with it, like all of us, and now we all had work to do to make up for it with

Sabine. If Jude's was the harder road, that was ultimately his problem.

I walked into the lobby and entered the elevator, pressing the button and closing my eyes as the doors closed. *Focus. She will need me at my intellectual peak if I am to be of help to her.*

The problem was, I knew that no matter how much I concentrated, I would face yet another distraction once I reached her room...her.

Laying my detachment aside and showing her the truth of me would leave me even more vulnerable to her charms, which were prodigious.

I leaned against the wall of the elevator as it slowly ground its way upward. When I closed my eyes, my eidetic memory turned into a curse—every part of her haunted me. Her voice, her face, her hair, her delicate scent when she had brushed past me on her way to the door. The way her hips swayed when she walked. Those bottomless dark eyes.

I couldn't control my body's response to her beauty or her fiery personality, and I struggled with my emotions. In her presence, it would be even more difficult. But I couldn't let that stop me. Otherwise, I would lose any chance I had to connect with her.

Nobody was in the hallway as I approached her door. I stepped up and rapped on it gently, saying almost at once, "Sabine? It's Nathaniel. I believe Blake told you I was coming."

For several heartbeats, there was nothing but silence, and I crushed down a surge of apprehension. She did not strike me as the flaky type, which meant that if she wasn't there, there had been another problem. But then I heard a creaking sound and footsteps padding toward the door. It unlocked, and Sabine peered out at me skeptically.

I caught her checking beyond me and nodded a bit sadly, knowing she had grown wary of every interaction at this school.

"Come in," she offered finally, and I nodded and followed her inside.

The room was small, neat, and dominated by her computer setup, complete with professional lights, a decent core system, and an enormous flat screen. It was almost as big as the one Jude used for his gaming. As I glanced around, I saw a tripod tucked inside the open closet and a newish camera sitting on a shelf near it. She only had one chair, the computer chair at her desk. Her bed was narrow, the bedspread plain, as were the curtains. Her upgrades to her space had been purely technological.

"Thanks for coming," she declared in a very neutral voice, her gaze searching my face. I felt that distracting surge of desire again and forced myself to do quadratic equations in my head until it went away. She noticed my distracted expression and frowned. "This is my one morning off, so let's get to it. How much time do you have?"

"Three hours until classes," I clarified. The classes in question were hardly ones I had to worry about. Anthropology and the single obligatory English class for general education requirements that I hadn't tested out of. In short, largely a waste of my time. If she turned out to need more help, I could skip them. "I can stay longer if needed."

Her eyebrow quirked, and she smiled faintly. "I only really need help in my general education courses. I have three of them, and I swear they're giving me fits. I'm still not sure why they're required."

"Well, the liberal arts department demands a certain amount of math and science. They consider it part of a well-rounded education. A common practice that I find tiresome. However, as a physics student, I should be especially able to help you study and prepare."

"Good. I got ambitious and took astrophysics, and the

professor is difficult. I swear that man talks like he grew up in a lab orbiting Jupiter and has only had human contact with other scientists since birth. I wrote down all his jargon, but it makes absolutely no sense to me." She went to her desk and pulled out a blue-covered notebook. "You can sit on the bed. I only have the one chair right now. They wouldn't let me keep the one I borrowed from the common room."

"Fine." It felt strange settling on the edge of her bed, feeling the overstuffed comforter give under me and smelling her perfume and soft, enticing, musky under-scent clinging to it. I surreptitiously adjusted the crotch of my trousers once she had handed me the notebook and then turned to go back to her chair. "Dr. Lambert?"

"Yes, the exact one. Why did you have him?" Her faint smile became an exasperated smirk.

"I had him my first year, when I was determining which aspects of physics I wished to focus on. He helped me decide against astrophysics." I tried on a small smile, touched by irony, and saw her blink in surprise. "He is the very definition of a lab rat. He never even bothers to correctly spell what he puts on the board. Apparently, when he coauthored the textbook, he left his editor in tears over his quirky spelling and grammar."

"Thank God it's not just me, then." She puffed out her cheeks and regarded me curiously. "You're a little different. Were you putting on an act as well that night?"

"A bit of one. I withdraw during conflict. I only emphasized it more than usual. Had I the choice, I would have boycotted the entire meeting." I hesitated, knowing that sounding too sincere after being so detached would seem fake to her. She was smart, observant, and understandably wary.

"I see." She sounded a touch startled. "You all just went along with what Blake wanted?"

"He is chapter president," I replied a little too quickly. "We voted him in for a reason, and we follow his lead for a reason. However, that does not mean his authority is unquestionable or that he doesn't make mistakes."

"Fair enough," she intoned. Her thoughtful stare told me she was chewing over this additional information and didn't quite know what to make of it yet. Then she pushed all that aside. "So, astrophysics."

"Yes, let me see here." I opened the notebook and started paging through, finding her notes thorough and in a much neater hand than Lambert's. "Well, you've taken down everything he said and wrote, though I'm afraid he's misspelled even some of his technical terms." It was almost painful to see those transcribed mistakes glaring from the page. The perfectionist in me wanted to fix all of them.

"Yes, I tried looking some of this up online to get a bit of insight, but no matter how hard I tried, I couldn't even find them with suggestions on." She winced.

"Let's start there, then. Your notes will do you no good if parts of them are incomprehensible." I grabbed a red pen and started the corrections, working quickly. "You may notice a few —" I paused, eyebrows climbing as I skimmed the gibberish written under the first diagram. "You wrote everything down word for word?"

"Yes. I even photographed the board so I could copy the diagrams correctly."

"I see. Well, he's mislabeled his own diagram." Instead of trying to fix it in the limited space, I took a gummed notepad from my pocket, drew the corrected diagram onto it, and then pasted the corrected one over her copy. "There. That should be a great deal more comprehensible."

She peered at it, then nodded, looking relieved. "And here I thought I was just stupid or something."

"Far from it. The man is misleading his entire classroom

with jargon, poor spelling, and mis-drawn diagrams. He'll have dozens of students failing the midterm because of his own mistakes." I couldn't keep the warmth out of my voice as I spoke to her. But when I took back the notebook, I saw that her smile had returned.

We went on like that. Once she realized that the problem was with the professor and not with her ability to understand the material, she immediately did a lot better. "So, this rule for calculating the distance of galaxies according to their redshift— is this written correctly?"

"No. The Hubble law in question is not a strict ratio. It is that same ratio, minus one." I added that to the equation, squinting in disgust. Lambert was a dinosaur, one of the oldest members of the science faculty. And as we went on, the sheer number of stupid mistakes made me wonder if his mind was going. "You know, I'm actually serious about his setting your classmates up to fail. This is going to lead to a very large number of angry students addressing the dean of sciences next week."

She sighed and nodded, biting her lip. "We have one more class before the midterm. I'm wondering if I shouldn't pass out the collected notes with a little memo."

"What sort of memo?" I struggled with the growing sense of affection I felt as I gazed at her. I had gone from wanting to impress her intellectually to wanting to touch her, and it had barely been an hour. *Focus, damn you. She needs your full abilities, not you turning into a horny fool after only an hour.*

"Hmm." She tapped her gleaming lips with a finger. "Something like, 'I have corrected these notes, including the diagrams, with the aid of an upperclassman in physics.' Then include the photos of the board so they can verify that he messed up, and I didn't just mis-transcribe."

"That could make you some friends in your astrophysics

class. For those students, the warning alone could be a life-saver. How do you plan to prevent Lambert from finding out? He's extraordinarily proud." I felt a stab of apprehension at the prospect of her getting on the nasty side of the faculty, on top of everything else. Lambert had been especially furious in his online screeds against not only allowing Sabine to attend, but even allowing women to be on faculty. He would need little provocation to provide Sabine with a fresh set of problems.

"There's an email list for the class. I can copy the emails on the list and make sure that Lambert's isn't among them, then cc everyone." Her expression was apprehensive. "Do you think some asshole in the class will forward it to him?"

"Hmm." I hated to admit it, but it was a possibility. And Lambert's tantrum wasn't something I wanted her to deal with. But still... "Perhaps. However, those who do not heed your warning are going to fail, and badly, and then Lambert will end up in trouble with his dean. Anything he tries to do against you to retaliate will make him look that much worse."

"Oh. Wow. Well, okay. Then I'm going to take the risk and go for it. I can't just stand by and let everyone end up failing because the prof screwed up."

I was smiling too much. I couldn't help it. "You know, you're extraordinary."

"Sorry?" she asked, a bright little laugh in her voice.

"You have every reason to want to stand by and let the men in your astrophysics class fall flat on their faces. I'm certain some of your antagonists are among them." At her nod, I sighed. "Yes, I thought so. And yet, instead of seeking revenge through simple inaction, you're trying to help them."

"This has never been about revenge," she murmured as she paged through the notes we had worked so hard to correct. "I didn't set out to pick a fight with anyone. I respond when it happens, because I don't lie down when someone tries to bully me."

"Yes, well, something like this will undermine your detractors' arguments by a great deal." I stood up as she did and watched her stretch and work the stiffness from her slim shoulders. My groin ached, and I ached with the need to touch her.

"I guess it will. I'm mostly thinking about not letting everyone fail because the teacher's an idiot at communicating concepts." She frowned. "He shouldn't be in teaching if he's going to do things like this. Is there any chance he'll correct himself once the dean speaks to him?"

I shook my head, too aware of how close she was. I wanted to run my fingers through her hair. She astonished me. Fascinated me. And it was getting more and more difficult to ignore that in favor of academics.

I took a huge breath. "Do you wish to go on to the next subject, or do you need a break?"

"Let's plow on. That one was the worst. My calculus class should be a breeze next to it, and by comparison with those two, my English lit class won't take much work at all." She paused, gazing up at me, and then swallowed and glanced away as she sat back down and reached for a red-covered notebook.

She was shy when I got close to her. There was something achingly flattering about it. *Did she feel the same attraction that I did? Was I that fortunate?*

I forced myself back to work, diving into the warmly familiar waters of calculus, at least Professor Ogata knew both her subject and how to spell—and teach. I pored over Sabine's notes quietly for a while, then peered up. "Well, there are no issues with your notes. Is there any aspect of the covered material that you feel less confident in?"

She gave me a genuine smile then. "Mostly the second half.

I grasped the basic concepts, but some of these equations are driving me crazy."

I did my best to help, teaching her some simple tricks for remembering and practicing the equations in question. "She has laid out the course so that each section builds on the last. Unfortunately, one's grasp of the basics only helps with the advanced concepts, not in memorizing the equations."

"Yeah, rote memorization has never been one of my strong points. I'm guessing they don't allow open-book or open-notes exams much at this school." She looked just a touch frustrated, and I felt my stomach tighten. I wanted to make it better. But the only way to do that, realistically, was to stay focused and do exactly as I was doing.

"Not in the beginner classes. The professors wish to ensure that you have fully understood the basic concepts before filling up your head with things so complex, one would have difficulty memorizing them at all." I laid my hand on her shoulder. She blinked at me. I withdrew it. "Sorry," I murmured. "That was likely presumptuous."

She scoffed gently. "You're an interesting guy, Nathaniel. Way different from what I expected. In a good way," she reassured me. "I would have ended up on Lambert's list of casualties without you."

She hadn't mentioned the hand on her shoulder. I drew a sharp breath, excited by this discovery. If it had bothered her, she would have said something.

"It's my pleasure to be of help to you," I murmured, feeling foolish but giving up on hiding my feelings. "I wanted to present a better impression of myself, and of us. You don't hate us, do you?"

She laughed out loud. "No. I don't hate you. You've been working with me for two solid hours trying to fix things. I'm glad you came," she admitted, a little more softly, her eyes holding my gaze.

"I'm glad to hear that I have made a better impression today," I responded. We were both standing again, facing each other. Very close. *When had that happened?* "You hating me, or thinking I felt anything for you besides admiration and desire..."

"Desire?" she asked softly. Something in her low, husky voice left me hard and aching even worse than before.

"I can't deny it," I expressed breathlessly. "Nor do I wish to."

She swallowed hard with her face tilted up toward mine. When I moved forward, she didn't draw back or tell me to stop.

I was tasting her lips against mine, feeling their silkiness slide against my own, before I knew what was happening. When I felt her respond, and her hands slide up my chest, I forgot all about self-control.

CHAPTER 15

SABINE

SOMETHING HAD SNAPPED INSIDE ME. It was the only way I could describe it. Daniel flirted with me. I had agreed to a date with Blake, but this was different. Far different.

What had turned me on the most, when I got down to it, had been watching Nathaniel struggle against his obvious desire while he had spent two and a half hours tutoring me. All the while, he had wanted to touch me. I had watched his hands flex at his sides; I had watched him shudder when I got near him; I had watched his eyes dilate and his cock press against the front of his trousers so insistently that all the surreptitious adjusting he'd done when he'd thought I wasn't paying attention hadn't done a thing to conceal it.

Maybe I was just a little sadistic for watching him agonize like that, but it had turned me on. I had spent half the time we had been together pressing my thighs together hard to fight against the hot throbbing of my cunt. With midterms on the line, I, too, had been forced to keep desire from distracting me. But now, my lust was ablaze at his reaction to me. It was more than flattering. It was primal. He had genuinely helped me, and left to himself, with none of the others to pressure him, he had been more than decent. When we had finally kissed, I'd felt a magnetic, incendiary connection, and everything after that, until this moment, was a delicious blur.

My blouse and bra were off as I lay back, his lips and tongue working against my nipple. I moaned, writhing under him as he crouched over me. My comforter rustled softly beneath me as he pulled seductively at my nipple. He flicked his tongue rapidly against my flesh, sending electric jolts outward from my breast, down between my thighs, where my aching pussy pulsed with emptiness. I clenched my fingers hard into the sheet while I arched and gasped encouragement, the other hand lost in his thick, dark hair.

I should have been more cautious and ashamed. But I had decided I wanted this a while ago when I had bought condoms on my way home after Blake had nailed down a date with me. I had decided it when I had kissed Nathaniel back. I had decided it when I had let him take off my blouse and bra, laying me down on the bed, kissing me hungrily. I wanted him.

Propped up on one hand, he worked my other nipple with his fingers in time with the lashing of his tongue. I sobbed and pumped my hips.

"Oh, it's good," I whimpered, body moving along with the long pulls of his mouth as he hovered over me, his knees on either side of my hips. "Oh, don't stop,"

I couldn't control the sounds I was making. I didn't want to. When he trailed his hand down to my belt buckle, I didn't freeze up, and I didn't tell him to stop. Instead, I trembled with anticipation as he pulled my zipper down and eased the jeans over my hips. "Oh yes," I whimpered. "Yes."

He slid his hand inside my panties, cupping my mound and kneading it firmly. My aching clit tingled sharply with each squeeze. I cried out, squirming, voice rising to desperate sobs as he drove the heel of his hand against my mound lightly with each caress. Nobody had ever touched me there. I had barely touched myself there. But I feared his stopping more than almost anything in the world.

He switched nipples, nibbling softly before settling in to suck me in strong strokes. I felt my cunt tighten, hungry to be filled. "Oh." I felt a fluttering sensation starting between my thighs as my muscles tightened.

Kissing had become caressing each other, then his kissing my neck, and then his mouth skating down to my breast. I wanted that pleasure. Ravenous, I squirmed and shimmied against his hand, my body starting to tingle all over. Every muscle in my body was tightening. I pulled him closer. He grunted softly and moved his hand and mouth faster while I answered with a heartfelt croon.

It was almost agonizing. I needed more, but I didn't know if I could stand it. Desperate, I ground against his hand, sobbing wordlessly. He paused for a painful second and then removed his hand from my panties.

I groaned through my teeth, furious at him for stopping, and moaned, "No, no, more, please."

I felt his lips curve into a smile around my nipple, and he slipped his hand back inside my panties.

Two slim fingers slid in between my pussy lips at once and started stroking up and down, slowly at first, mapping me from the opening of my cunt to the burning kernel at the top of my slit. I hitched my hips against him harder, crooning almost soundlessly, and felt him move upward more and more until his fingers delicately tapped against either side of my clit.

"Oh!" I sobbed. "Oh, oh! Yes!"

He moved his mouth against me, matching the rhythm of his fingers, slow at first, then faster, ramping up gradually while I begged for him to finish me. I had never felt anything this good, but I couldn't stand it anymore either. "Do it, do it, do it," I heard myself whimpering as he started flicking his fingers faster and faster.

My voice was out of control, the cries that came out of me loud enough to echo off the walls. It was so good that I almost couldn't take it. "Please," I whimpered, then shouted it. "Please! Ah!"

He held steady, flicking my clit with delicate ferocity until I felt every muscle in my body tighten. I went up on my heels, my cunt clenching like a fist—and then releasing in rippling waves as ecstasy tore through me again and again.

I heard myself screaming with joy, and then it was ending, drying up, the contractions weakening to delightful aftershocks as I collapsed limply on the bed. Eyes huge, I stared at the ceiling, gasping for breath so hard I couldn't speak.

Nathaniel's eyes were burning as he raised his head. Almost blind with lust, he climbed off me and stripped. His leanly muscled body gleamed like marble. His enormous cock caught me off guard. I hadn't expected the Gentlemen's resident nerd to be hung or shaved. But Nathaniel was both.

Chest heaving, he reached for his briefcase and fumbled with it, then examined me, eyes burning with blind lust. "Condoms?"

"Bedside drawer," I managed as I hastily tore off the rest of my clothes. I had never felt such satisfaction as I did right then —but the sight of him made me want more. It made me want his cock.

He found one and rolled it on with shaking hands. I watched the purple tip of his cock disappear under the latex. When he finished rolling on the condom, he climbed over me again, and I opened my arms and thighs for him eagerly.

He groaned through his teeth as he slid into me then met

the resistance of my tightness. "Sabine," he gasped out. "I didn't know..."

"Do it," I moaned.

He lifted his hips and then pushed down again firmly. I felt momentary pain that was promptly replaced with pleasure. I wrapped my arms and thighs around him and lifted my hips to take it as he thrust slowly, trying to savor the moment even as he shuddered and panted with need.

He sped up, thrusting faster and harder, his lean belly bumping against mine as he fucked me. His face transformed. Stoicism gone, his eyes wide and his lips parted as he rolled his hips against me faster and faster. I felt the pressure of his hips against mine, and it sent me up the ramp again. My clit tingled sharply when our bellies slapped together, and both my hands were in his hair. I watched him struggle to hold out as the delicious, unfamiliar sensation of his cock caressed me roughly from within. He was silent except for his shuddering gasps.

I shimmied my hips harder. He let out a grunt, then moaned softly and thrust harder. His entire body was taut with pleasure. When I ran my nails over his ass, the muscles were so tight they felt like stone. We trembled together, panting, until finally, his head swung away from me as his back arched.

"Oh!" His sharp shouts turned me on even more. I ground harder and grinned when he responded with a desperate-sounding moan. My body took off again as he started pounding faster and faster. I squealed and rose up on my heels, while he grunted and gasped and then finally shouted, deep and intense, every time he drove his cock into me.

My body stayed keyed up as he pounded into me as fast as he could, the entire bed shaking under us. I dug my nails into his ass as he arched harder and his shouts interspersed with desperate pants. "Coming," he gasped out suddenly. "Sabine!"

He drove his cock deep into me, and I felt it spasm. His

eyes squeezed closed, and he grabbed both my hips, pulling them up close to him as he writhed against me. His shaft bucked inside me again and again as he squirmed over me. His face was tight with ecstasy. Then gradually, it ended, and he collapsed over me, trembling and gasping for breath.

I drifted, more relaxed than I had ever been with another person in the room. Part of me was a little shocked with myself, but that voice in the back of my head that wanted to tell me I had taken a colossal risk was barely audible now. Contented, I closed my eyes.

When I opened them again, Nathaniel had gone to my attached bathroom to rid himself of the condom. He returned, still unselfconsciously nude. His skin was flushed, his cock still at half-mast, and his eyes gleamed as he eyed me.

Suddenly self-conscious, I glanced down at myself, to discover he had folded one side of the comforter over me. I didn't realize why until I glanced through the slats of the window beside me and realized that it was snowing again. Even with the comforter over me, my nipples were tight from the chill. Had I lost time? "I dozed off," I mumbled.

"For a little while." He sounded almost smug, and I lifted an eyebrow before sighing and lounging back against my pillow.

He paused, then moved toward me and settled on the edge of the bed, ignoring the cold. "Are you all right?"

I blinked up at him, then sat up again, drawing my knees to my chest, wrapping the comforter around me and settling my head on my knees.

"I'm just not used to this," I mumbled.

"Why didn't you tell me you were a virgin?" He brushed his fingers over my exposed shoulder, and I shivered, my skin tingling.

"I didn't want to make a big deal about it."

"Thank you for allowing me to be your first, Sabine." He kissed me gently.

I swallowed hard, wondering why my eyes were suddenly stinging from restraining tears. It took me a little while of searching myself as he slid behind me on the bed, but finally, I grasped it. It was the feeling I got when I came in from the cold and only then realized how chilled I had gotten. The feeling was something I had been denying ever since I had come to this place. Loneliness. Sexual frustration, I was used to. All those weeks of slogging through everything alone, with only Billy, Mom, and a few blog fans to break my isolation, had taken a slow and unhappy toll on me.

I closed my eyes, feeling my lashes grow damp, and went quiet as I struggled with my emotions. "I've been alone a lot," I admitted finally. "Ever since I came here. I have one friend, one. And all these people trying to force me out. I'm strong, but..." But not invulnerable. People weren't meant to deal with this much isolation.

"I'm sorry." He wrapped his arms around me, his long limbs well up to the task without squeezing me too hard. "Most of the students must have been terrible. We've been terrible too."

"Yeah. And now you're not. You're the opposite, and I'm just trying to adjust." And in doing so, I had to face facts. I had to face just how much having almost everyone try to push me out had hurt. I shivered.

His grip tightened on me. "It will be all right," he promised me.

I gulped and nodded slightly, but the comfort made the contrast between now and what I had gone through all that much sharper.

He wasn't shivering or complaining about the chill next to the window, but I could see gooseflesh rising on his forearms. I let him in under the comforter, and we cuddled for a while, bare skin warm against bare skin. Now and again, his breath blew hot against the back of my neck, stirring up a fresh tingle that ran throughout my body.

"Thank you," I offered once the pain inside had subsided a little. "For everything. I'm glad you came over." Weird that I had seen him as some cold asshole before. He still seemed almost unnervingly stoic and calm, but now, I knew better. And I was glad to have met the man he was behind that.

"I'm happy to have helped, but I fear I've disrupted your study session." I felt his chuckle against my back more than heard it. "I should probably get going before I disrupt your day further."

Suddenly, the loneliness inside yawned open again like a wound. I grabbed his forearms and hung on to them, and he went still. "Only if you want to," I whispered.

He was quiet for a few seconds. "I don't want to. I would rather order pizza and then make love to you again."

I pulled away just enough to stare at him. "Then do it."

He smiled slowly. "If that is what you wish."

"It is." My heart was pounding. I'd hate being left alone when I felt this vulnerable.

He snuggled up to me again and kissed the back of my neck. "Your wish is my command."

CHAPTER 16

BLAKE

"YOU SON OF A BITCH!" The words came out of me all on their own, before I even realized how angry I was.

Nathaniel stared back at me, his expression damnably placid. "Please calm down," he said. "There's really no reason for you to be so upset."

"No reason?" Never in all our years of knowing each other had I wanted to punch him in the teeth this badly. He was standing there smugly in the door to the entry hall, bag over his shoulder, acting like nothing wrong had happened, like I was being unreasonable. But I knew the truth now, as did the others, and Nathaniel was going to answer for it.

Nathaniel had gone to Sabine's dorm to tutor her prior to midterms. He had then completely disappeared for almost two days. When he had returned, he had been strangely quiet and very exhausted. I had suspected something then, but I had kept my counsel until I was certain.

But then Sabine had disappeared on me. Not returning my calls, not returning my texts, and I could hardly bother her during class with midterms on. Now, days later, after putting together the pieces about why Sabine had postponed our date and was avoiding talking to me, I had confronted Nathaniel, and he had admitted it.

The son of a bitch had beaten me to her. He had cut in line. He had caused her to skip a date with me after taking her virginity. He had forgotten who was head of the pack around here, and it pissed me off to no end. And then, his only response, after he had stolen what should have been my time with Sabine, was to tell me to calm down.

Forget punching him. I wanted to kill him.

"I had a date with her. I was all set up to have time alone with her. I was first in line. She skipped our date to be with you! That's why she hasn't been returning my calls. I just found out for certain. She confessed to me to try to clear the air. What the hell were you thinking?" I couldn't keep my voice down. I was just too fucking furious.

"Yeah, man. That really wasn't cool." Marcus stood behind me, arms folded. I could tell he was seething, but he kept his voice a lot calmer than mine. "This isn't a competition, and you jumped the line."

"Excuse me?" Nathaniel scoffed. "We weren't in line for the ice cream man. She chose to be with me, and she postponed your date with her so we could continue." And from the big, smug smile on his face, he wasn't sorry at all. Not one bit. Hell, this was the first time I had seen a smile that wide on his face at all.

"That's not the point!" I moved closer to him, fists balled at my sides. His eyes narrowed slightly and his smile faded, but he stood his ground. I stopped short and poked a finger at his chest. "You knew I had a date with her. You got her to cancel, and to have an affair with you, without considering the insult to me."

"Insult?" He blinked at me with shock in his eyes. "It

occurs to me that if anything, you are the one who is insulting her."

I drew back my hand, folding my arms and shifting my weight. Behind me on one of the common room couches, Jude sat forward, making the cushion rustle slightly. "How do you figure?" Jude asked skeptically. "I mean, we had an agreement here. You were supposed to meet her for tutoring, not fucking."

Nathaniel shrugged. "I did not get Sabine to do anything. I did not take control of her and cause her to sleep with me, and I did not make the choice for her to postpone your date." He was still damnably calm. "Nor did I have any say in her not calling you back. I wasn't even aware of it until you brought it up now. She made those choices, as she is, you know, a free individual and not a passive object."

"Oh, fuck you, Nathaniel," Marcus sighed in exasperation as I dug my nails into the flesh of my palms. "It's not like we're fighting over her like a piece of meat. You know what Blake is talking about."

Nathaniel hung up his bag and walked past me, sitting down in one armchair. "No," he replied, voice still infuriatingly calm. "I don't. And given his behavior, that seems to be exactly what he is doing. What you're doing, to a lesser degree. You should ask her why she skipped your date, not scream at me as if her free choice was a plot to undermine your precious authority."

I stiffened, moving closer to the group, arms shaking with the urge to lift him up by his collar. I deliberately kept out of arm's reach so I wouldn't be tempted. "I do not treat her like a piece of meat."

"No," Nathaniel replied. "But you are treating her like a possession. Your possession."

"What is going on?" Daniel yawned on his way down the main stairs. His hair was mussed, and he was still buttoning his shirt. I shot him a disapproving glare. He ignored it, annoying me even more than I already was. "I heard yelling."

"Blake is having a fit of jealousy," Nathaniel disclosed.

Marcus huffed a sigh. "Stop being a dick, Nathaniel."

"I'm not." He turned back to me, lifting an eyebrow. "I am being honest. I keep trying to tell you, Sabine is her own woman—not yours, mine, or anyone's. She chose everything that happened. I did not manipulate her into spending time with me."

That just made my blood boil more. *How in the hell could he be so nonchalant about all this? And how could he call me the immature one in this situation, when he had turned a tutoring session into a seduction and gotten his dick in before I could even get my date?*

Jude shrugged. "Dude. That's true. Nate here couldn't manipulate his way out of a wet paper bag. And besides—"

"Shut up!" I barked over my shoulder. Somewhere in the back of my mind, behind the rage, a small voice nagged that maybe I was overreacting and taking all this way too personally. But I hated being ignored and disregarded. I hated being put second and disobeyed.

"Whoa," Daniel muttered and went to sit by Jude. "Okay, I definitely missed something."

"Dude's pissed off because Sabine went and fucked Nathaniel after their study date," Jude explained with his usual lack of tact. "She also broke a date with Blake the next day."

"Shit," Daniel sighed as he flopped down into a chair, his shirt hanging open negligently across his broad chest. "Well, shouldn't you be bitching at her instead of at Nathaniel?" His accent was thicker when he was half asleep. I wondered what he had been doing all night. Had he been with her too?

I considered that, then shook my head. "This isn't about the choices Sabine makes as far as bed partners." *Yes, it is,* but saying that wouldn't get me a good reaction right now. I stood with my back to the entryway, arms folded, with Marcus coming to stand next to me. "This is about Nathaniel knowing that I was first. As is right."

"Why is it right?" Nathaniel asked mildly. "You're the head of fraternity leadership. The matter with Sabine is different. It is personal. I do not think your rationale respects her autonomy very much at all."

"You're only talking about her 'autonomy' because it worked out in your favor." I forced myself to turn to Daniel. "The issue is largely that Sabine broke the date. I should bring it up with her, and I will. Meanwhile, my argument stands. Nathaniel should have had the consideration to back off until I had at least had my date with her."

Nathaniel stared back at me. "I didn't go in there planning to fuck her, Blake. You're being paranoid. It happened."

"What, did you somehow fall out of your clothes and fall on top of her several times? For days?" My voice rose to a shout of outrage.

Jude, Daniel, and Nathaniel went quiet suddenly and stared past me. Marcus frowned and then turned to see what they were observing. After a brief struggle, I curbed my rage and peered over my shoulder.

Carmody was standing in the entryway, staring at us, eyes and mouth both wide in shock and horror.

Oh shit. My heart sank. Of all the times for the crazy bastard to come wandering in searching for more free food, he had to choose now. "This is a private conversation, Carmody. Breakfast finished an hour ago."

He just stared at me. "You..." he started. "Dates? Sex? You're fucking that interloping cunt?" His voice rose in absolute outrage. "You said you hadn't touched her."

"None of this is your business, Mikey," Marcus warned, but I had already lost my temper.

I advanced on him, face burning, fingernails biting into my palms so hard they stung.

"We're trying to save our school, and you bastards are letting her manipulate you with her pussy!" Carmody yelled.

"Get out!" I roared, lunging forward and grabbing him by the front of his battered trench coat. "Take your aging ass and go somewhere where you're wanted, if that place exists outside your mother's basement!" I shoved him hard toward the door. He flailed, suddenly conscious that he was being kicked out. "It's none of your business how we handle the Sabine situation. You're just a fucking pledge, and that's all you'll ever be. You're not part of leadership. You're not even part of the fraternity. Now get out before we fucking ban you."

He stumbled away from me, face going from red to white and back again. "Looks like she's the one running this fraternity —with her pus—" He didn't even have time to finish his accusation. I raised a fist, and he darted for the door and ran out.

"Fuck!" I snarled as I locked the door behind him. The members had keys. The pledges could fucking well knock from now on.

"That was unfortunate," Nathaniel mumbled, sounding more concerned about Carmody's intrusion than he was about my anger.

I turned back to him, scowling. "Next time I tell you I have a date with Sabine, keep your dick to yourself until it's done. If you interrupt again..."

"Again, with the not respecting her choices," Nathaniel replied, having the balls to be annoyed with me.

"Just do it," I snarled. "If we're going to share her, we need to do it in a way that doesn't step on one another. I'm pissed at her for skipping out on our date and then ignoring my calls for almost a week."

"Part of that was getting through midterms, likely," Daniel pointed out.

Goddamn it. I silently counted to twenty and then sighed. "Okay, there is that. But she's such a damn bookworm that studies getting in the way will always be a thing. I can handle that. I can't handle this fucking betrayal."

"That wasn't the intention," Nathaniel protested, but his voice was quiet now, and he sounded almost contrite.

"Whether done intentionally or thoughtlessly, the results were the same. Not all of us are experienced with polyamory, and not all of us have sorted out situations like this before. The whole thing depends on communication and respect. The least we can do is adhere to a schedule with one another and respect the agreed-upon rules."

"All right. That I can go along with. I apologize for my part in ruining your date." Nathaniel peered over at the coffee machine and then went over to pour himself a cup. "Perhaps I should have caffeinated before coming back here."

"Me too," Daniel agreed, getting up to wait for Nathaniel to finish. "Maybe that would have helped me figure out what was up faster. Do you think Carmody will do anything with his new knowledge?" His expression was concerned.

"I don't care," I muttered. "Anything that childish idiot throws at us, we can handle."

After finishing up at the fraternity house, I checked my copy of Sabine's schedule. She had no afternoon classes until late, which meant she would eat, then retire to her dorm room as usual to study, work on her vlog, or get in a nap. She was a creature of habit, like me. I liked that about her. It made catching up with her just that much easier.

Outside, it was still below freezing, thin berms of hard

snow piled up against every curb. It was too early for this kind of weather. I hoped the next five-odd months wouldn't pass exactly the same way.

No sign of Carmody. He had already scuttled away in the fifteen minutes it had taken me to finish my conversation, fortify myself with coffee, and then put on my coat and boots. I wasn't worried about him. The man was a coward to the bone, which was one reason for his total lack of success with women, and with life.

Despite the cold, I walked across campus to Sabine's dorm. I had a lot of anger to burn off, and I didn't want to bring it to her. I tried never to scream at women. The last thing I wanted was to scare her off. But we needed to clear the air between us.

I only hoped she wasn't actually monogamous. If she had fixated on Nathaniel instead of me, I wasn't sure I could ever really forgive him.

CHAPTER 17

SABINE

"YEAH, Mama, I survived all my midterms. Just started getting my grades back. Ninety-plus percent on all tests and projects. I'm killing it!" I felt proud.

"Good, good. You sounded so stressed out the week before that I thought I would have to drag you away from your studies personally." She paused. "Have the men there stopped bothering you?"

"Most of them, yeah. There are a few holdouts, like that Carmody guy we ran into on the way in. But most of them have gotten used to me being here. I've even made a few friends." I was on the fence about gushing over Nathaniel. She was anxious about my safety on campus, and she had always scrutinized every single guy who had ever approached me for a date.

Instead, I told her about one result of our time together. "It helps that I kind of helped save everybody's grade in my astrophysics class."

"Oh? How did that happen?" She sounded a little excited. It was one of the first times she had since the weather had turned bad. Her depression always got worse the colder and darker it got. At least the money I had sent was helping her deal with the dreariness and deep cold of what seemed to be an eerily premature winter.

I told her about all the errors in the professor's materials that Nathaniel and I had found. "So basically, I got on the class mailing list, excluded the professor, and warned them all. And I gave them the corrected information we had come up with." I was proud as hell about it. Nathaniel was right—I could have just let all those guys twist in the wind in response to how they had treated me. But the results had been more than worth the extra effort.

"How did they respond when you helped them like that? I know many of them were against your going at all." She sounded a little skeptical—like she thought I was trying too hard. I couldn't blame her. I had nearly avoided going through with it out of a mix of overcaution and spite. But I had, and the results had thrilled me.

"Some of them said thanks, and that was it. Some of them have stayed quiet. One accused me of being a kiss-ass, but he's a friend of Carmody's, so I didn't think much of it. But some others, well, it was amazing." I took a deep breath. It was now four days after the astrophysics email, and I was still getting reactions. Positive ones.

"What did they do? Don't leave me hanging here, child!" she scolded cheerfully.

I laughed. "Well, some of them asked why I had done it, and I said they were my classmates and not doing so felt like cheating instead of healthy competition." They had confronted me in class, four of them, one of them wearing an Alpha Omega pin. "I don't think they were expecting me to care. But they seemed glad that I did."

"Good! I didn't raise you to be nasty or a cheat. So, have they been troubling you since then?"

I winced slightly. I had finally come clean about some problems I was having. Mom didn't follow my blog that often because of a lack of connectivity, but she had seen my settling-in post with the note on the wall, and that had led to a discussion. But I was still keeping the bulk of my worries from her, knowing she'd take it way harder than she needed to in her current condition. "Not in that class. Carmody's still out in the snowstorm outside my dorm waving a sign, like I said, but he is down to about half a dozen guys. As for online, well, my fans have my back, and some have even sent some more donations."

That part, I didn't know what to think about. There was a tidy pile of money waiting in my donation account, enough that I could have a down payment on a car together soon. It tempted me to just get a bike and muddle through while helping my mom out more and investing most of the rest. I wanted to be smart, and even as chilly as it was out here for a third of the year, the bike would serve me just as well most of the time.

"Oh, that's lovely! Now, don't you go handing it all to me. You have your own needs." She was scolding me preemptively. I laughed a little.

"Oh, Mama, don't worry about that. Your being healthy and happy is one of my needs. Anyway, I'm saving nearly all of it until I figure out what to do."

I suddenly heard a firm knock at my door, different from Nathaniel's gentle rapping. "Looks like I've got a visitor." I sighed. "I'll call you back."

"Visitor? Good. You spend too much time alone over there. If it's Billy, say hello for me, all right?"

"I will, Mama. I love you." I ended our call just as the knock came again. "Hold on," I called out cheerfully, walking to the door. I peered out the peephole, and my cheerful smile fled.

It was Blake. And he did not look pleased.

I sighed, then braced myself and unlocked the door. He had every reason to be angry with me. I had broken our date, then stopped returning his phone calls. I had good reasons for both, but I owed him the full explanation. Not just the half-assed apology I had made over the phone last night.

"Hi," I breathed.

"We need to talk," he demanded.

"I know," I replied softly. "Come in. Let's not do this out in the hallway."

I let him in and locked the door. "I'm sure you're pissed at me," I blurted before he could start. I went over to my bed and sat on its edge, offering him the chair. "You have a right to be. I hope you don't hate me."

He blinked in surprise and then scoffed. "If I hated you, I would dismiss you. You would never hear from me again."

"Well, then I'm doubly glad you're here. I want to clear the air. And when we last talked, I hadn't slept for two days." My eyes searched his face. He searched mine. "Part of why I wasn't up to explaining myself."

He tensed slightly. "Why? Nathaniel?"

"That's only part of it. And not in the way you mean. We haven't seen each other in almost a week. I needed to recover from midterms. I got the worst goddamn flu right at the end of exams. Got everything turned in and got good grades, but then I crashed hard." I winced apologetically at him as he settled into my computer chair.

His body relaxed. "I thought you were avoiding me."

"I kind of was," I admitted. "Once I realized I had missed our date, I didn't know what to do. I'm new at dating."

He sat back in the chair, blinking rapidly as he folded his arms. "Sorry? I don't understand." He seemed incredulous that I hadn't had a serious relationship before.

"I've never had a steady boyfriend. Now you and

Nathaniel and three other guys, all of whom have closer relationships with one another than with me, want to date me. Seriously." My cheeks got a little warm.

"Very seriously," he affirmed in a deeper, softer voice, gaze holding mine.

I swallowed. "Yeah, well, that's like someone throwing me into the deep end when I'm used to kiddie pools, okay? I didn't know how to handle it. I kind of still don't. I know I fucked up. I didn't mean to, but...I still did." And even though I had been overwhelmed by my encounters with Nathaniel and then midterms and then getting sick, I wanted to be a grown-up about dealing with all this.

He nodded slowly, thoughtfully, his intense eyes narrowed in contemplation. "Do you have second thoughts about us courting you? Because I'm concerned that Nathaniel's ruined things."

"No," I blurted and then more firmly said, "No. He's fine. I think he was caught off guard too, but he's given me the space I needed since then. I'm the one not handling things well."

If someone had told me three weeks ago that I would end up apologizing to Blake for anything at all, I would have laughed. He had been such an asshole when I had first met him, charming and sexy or not. I had learned better, especially about both him and Nathaniel in the last few weeks, but before then, I'd been convinced they were just a part of the forces aligned against me.

Now, I worried that I had hurt Blake terribly without even meaning to.

He didn't look hurt, though. More thoughtful and less pissed off. "Interesting. So, Nathaniel... He wasn't trying to monopolize your time?" His gaze had gone penetrating again.

"No, it wasn't like that. Honestly, I think he's as surprised as I am by what happened. I don't usually... I mean..." It felt awkward to talk about fucking Nathaniel. "I don't miss appointments," I pushed out in a desperate save. "And I sure don't miss dates, not usually."

"No, you didn't strike me as the type," he mused. "The question is, what do we do about it now?"

"Well, I'd like to try again. If you would." My stomach fluttered.

Then, finally, he smiled brilliantly, like a flash of lightning in the dark. "Very well. However, I may have to punish you a little, if you want to get back in my good graces." His wink told me he wasn't entirely serious—but the heat in his eyes told another story.

That heat wasn't anger. Not this time. And that left my stomach fluttering for another reason. A wonderful, delicious reason.

"Say the word, and I'll drop everything and go out with you tonight," I promised. "Though, that's not exactly a punishment."

He chuckled, low and husky. "Neither is what I have in mind. And yes, after what I'm thinking, you're definitely going to need an enormous meal."

Oh boy. I think I might be in the hottest kind of trouble. And there came that in-over-my-head feeling again. But I had experience in fighting off that fear now. I had fought it off when I had come here, during the harassment, and when Nathaniel had first kissed me. "Well, what do you have in mind?"

His grin was broad and wicked. "Something that I'm certain we both want."

I swallowed as he rose from his chair and bent over me, not even giving me time to stand before his mouth started ravishing mine. His kiss was rough, hungry, insistent. He pushed the cardigan of my little wool skirt suit off my shoulders and then shoved it down my arms, tossing it away. When his mouth trailed off to kiss the corner of my jaw instead, I gasped softly and let my head fall back into his cupped hands.

I realized what he wanted right away—control. Which was easy to give up when my inexperience and the power of my response put my thoughts on hold. His teeth grazed my neck. He nibbled and licked as he shucked his leather jacket, sending it to the floor with a heavy thump. He was stripping me again, unbuttoning my blouse and unbuckling my belt with one hand while the fingers of his other hand slid through my braids to grasp my scalp. I tried to help him out of his own clothes, but he fastened his mouth on me over my pulse and sucked hard, making me moan and rise against him.

In minutes, I was nude and he shirtless and without his boots, tossing my panties off into the corner and laying me back on the bed. His hungry kisses were working their way down my body, marking me with little suck marks, nipping, licking. I panted, hands sliding over his shoulders, only to have him take them both and lay them firmly on the mattress.

"Keep them there," he growled into my cleavage. "If you try to use them, I will tie you up."

I nodded frantically, panting, only hoping that he wouldn't stop.

His mouth didn't linger on my breasts like Nathaniel's had. Instead, he started kissing lower, leaving his trail of marks as I gasped and squirmed and dug all my fingers into the comforter. His lips grazed the top of my carefully trimmed pussy. He worked his fingers between my lower lips and parted them, holding them apart with his thumbs while two of his fingers slowly slid into me.

I sat up, whimpering, but somehow kept my hands down as he started licking me in long, lazy strokes. He took his time, exploring every curve and fold of me as his fingers stroked me from within, while my toes curled and my gasps and moans became more and more desperate.

Still, he teased me, over and over, caressing everything but my aching clit with his tongue. Every time he got near it, I thought he would finally give me relief, stimulating me just enough to let me climax. But every time, he teased me just long enough for my hips to lift and my voice to sob, "Yes," and then moved away again, caressing another part of my pussy instead.

He soon had me so turned on with all his teasing that my cunt clenched around his fingers so tight it almost hurt. My ass cheeks throbbed with tension. I dug my heels into the side of the bed. "Blake—" I sobbed finally, desperately.

And then, for a few terrible seconds, the magnificent bastard stopped. "Beg for it," he growled against me.

My chest heaved as he went back to teasing me, as my arousal got so strong that it edged on pain. The single scrap of pride that protested my begging for everything was incinerated in a firestorm of need. "Please!" I sobbed finally. "Please, Blake."

In response, he fastened his mouth over my clit and sucked.

I came immediately, screaming and thrashing, not caring if anyone in the other dorm rooms overheard. Every contraction exploded through me again and again, until I finally ran out of strength and collapsed, limp and trembling.

I had barely stopped screaming when I heard his belt hit the floor and the crinkling of a condom wrapper. Then he seized my legs, pulling my hips to the edge of the bed again, and thrust his cock into me roughly.

"Oh God, yeah," I groaned through my teeth as he started thrusting hard and fast, his eyes burning as he stared down at me. "Oh yeah, fuck me. Fuck me—harder!"

I moaned incoherently as he sped up, fingers digging into my hips as he lifted me against him. I circled my hips frantically, legs wrapped around him as he pounded into me. His cock was thicker than Nathaniel's and at least as long. If I weren't so turned on, it might have hurt—but as it was, I was so slick and relaxed and hungry for him I pushed myself up onto his thick shaft eagerly with every thrust.

He fucked me fiercely, his eyes blazing, his breath coming in harsh pants, his hips pounding against mine as he worked himself into me with all his strength. I felt myself getting turned on again, my satisfaction increasing with every slap of his hips to mine, driving us closer and closer to climax.

I moaned his name, and he growled incoherently, then closed his eyes and threw his head back. The movements of his hips became frantic. His hoarse calls got louder with each thrust until they drowned out my sobs of pleasure. I ground against him desperately—and rose to climax again, squealing with bliss, while he drove into me as deep as he could and came.

He roared with pleasure, his dick jumping inside me, spurting so hard that I could feel it through the condom. "Yes!" he shouted triumphantly. "Yes!" And then my own cries joined his as I unraveled with ecstasy around him.

The intimate little steak place, with giant photos of the best parts of the Catskills in the full flower of summer and rippled red candle-lanterns on every table, was the perfect place for a date. And after what Blake had spent hours doing to me, I was ravenous.

We were most of the way through our steaks when Blake declared, "Before I forget, I need to update you on something involving Carmody."

I tensed slightly, the luscious bite of prime rib in my mouth going dry. I swallowed hard. "What is it?"

His smile fled temporarily. "Thanks to some indiscretions this morning, he's aware that we're dating you. And he reacted badly."

Oh God. Not this shit. I had been hoping that Carmody would never realize we were together. Then again, it was a small campus, and he was pledging Alpha Omega and probably trying to have me watched. "What should I do?"

He smiled and reached across the table, enfolding my hand in his own. "Don't worry, we're handling this. In the meantime, if he comes near you, just call us."

"I'm putting you on speed dial, then." I shuddered slightly, despite the reassuring pressure of my lover's hand. "That guy, he makes me wish I owned a gun."

"Well, we'll be able to fast-track the conditional restraining order you wanted. And we'll handle the rest. He's losing followers by the day, especially after that coup you pulled in astrophysics." He sounded proud, which made me warm all over. "I believe that being yourself, with your high standards and strong ethics, will win over the rest."

"But Carmody, he's nuts," I breathed. "He doesn't just hate women, he's unstable and obsessed. You never really know what someone like that is going to do."

"He's a wimp. Once he loses all the freshmen he's been stirring up, he'll have no backup, and he's hardly got the nerve to try anything himself. Marcus is paying him a visit tomorrow to settle things. Try not to worry." He squeezed my hand again and then leaned back and let go to take up his wineglass. "Marcus can handle whatever Carmody tries to throw at him."

I hoped to God he was right. But I didn't let on about my doubts. I didn't want to ruin our lovely date with anything having to do with Carmody. Doing so felt like it was handing him a victory, and that, I swore to myself, could never happen.

Meanwhile, I had an even bigger problem to deal with. *How in the world was I going to juggle relationships with five guys, even if they knew about one another and were fine with it?*

Falling for them—except maybe Jude—would not be a problem. But how could I keep up all those relationships without screwing up—or ending up hurt myself?

CHAPTER 18

MARCUS

I KNEW something was up when I went to talk to Carmody at his dorm and discovered it stuffed full of guys I didn't recognize.

I didn't know if they were from off campus, or if they were just non-pledges I hadn't run into yet. But every one of them turned his head when I walked into the common room where he had agreed to meet and gave me the dead-eyed stare of a guy who thought he was facing an enemy.

"So, one of you finally showed up to explain yourself," Carmody declared as he sprawled spread-legged on one couch.

"No," I answered, keeping my smile on. "I'm here to deliver a warning."

One boy scoffed, and I turned to fix him with a stare. He was wearing a backward red ball cap and a T-shirt with a goddamn Guy Fawkes mask on it. "Did you go recruiting edge lords at the local high school or something?" I sneered, annoyed, as he wilted slightly under my gaze.

"It's none of your business where my supporters come from!" Carmody bellowed. "Say what you have to say and then go scuttling back to that bitch who is keeping your balls in her purse."

A chuckle ran around the room. I narrowed my eyes. "Fine, if you're going to be a little shit about it. The warning is this. Your constant escalation of harassment against Sabine is about to get you in some serious trouble if you don't stop. She's filing an emergency protection order against you, and she's already informed us that the next time any of you step over the line with her, she's involving the police."

The chuckling stopped dead, and Carmody closed his mouth with a meaty sound as he went a few shades paler. His smug expression wilted and died. "She wouldn't. That would get you and her other fucktoys in trouble."

Anger boiled inside me at his insults against me, my fraternity brothers, and Sabine, but I wouldn't give him the satisfaction of raising my voice. "As usual, you have it backward. You're not affiliated with Alpha Omega, so if you end up in jail for harassment or assault, it will be easy to deny any connection to you. You're just a pledge, Carmody. You're not even fraternity material. The only reason we have allowed you to camp out on our waiting list is because of daddy's money."

I paused before adding, "You also have it backward with Sabine."

He recovered slightly and glared at me. "How?" he asked, voice cracking. "How am I wrong?"

"It's simple. We're not her toys, she is ours. We have her completely in hand. That's why she has done no more negative reporting on the campus and why she's been quietly doing her work instead of sending the police after you already." I stared hard into his eyes until he blinked and glanced away. He feared the police. *Good.*

"As for opposing the administration's ham-handed move, we're going after them directly. With lawyers. Not by terrorizing the girl caught in the middle, not by threatening her family or friends, not by being sexist pieces of shit who eagerly break the law."

He tried on a smirk. "Well, that's awfully politically correct of you."

"Cuck," one kid with him said.

I turned on him, a skinny, colorless kid with an underbite and dull hazel eyes. "What, like your dad? From the looks of you, Mommy cheated on him with a salamander." The guy reddened and shut his mouth, glancing away.

I turned back to Carmody. "You shouldn't have been allowed to hang your maladjusted ass around our campus causing problems for so long. And now, you're about to go to jail because you're too thickheaded and full of hate to knock it off and focus on school. Or pledging. Or anything else. Meanwhile, we're handling this. The right way."

"Then why isn't she gone?" he screeched suddenly, exploding out of his seat, purple-faced, sweat breaking out all over him. "Why isn't that fucking idiot out of our space?"

"Because we don't take orders from you, pledge," I replied coldly. "Something you have conveniently forgotten repeatedly for years. But now? Now, you can fuck off."

His jaw dropped, and he started hyperventilating. "You can't throw me off the list. My father…"

"Your father's support hasn't been needed for years," I sighed. "And if you get yourself thrown in jail, you can't expect him to go to bat for you with us anyway."

His mouth worked as he slowly sat back down. "You're telling me this, why? To scare me away from your piece of ass?"

"To keep you from doing something so goddamned stupid that you end up in jail and drag your dumbass followers with you." I panned my eyes around. "You guys want to catch a record and maybe jail time for this dick? Think about it."

A few of them appeared doubtful, but most just glared back at me stubbornly. *Dumbass kids.* Carmody had gone and found himself the youngest, stupidest antifeminists he could to back him. I wondered if any of them were students here at all.

"My father has an excellent lawyer," Carmody scoffed. "And it will be hard to have me thrown in jail when I have witnesses handy who can say, for example, that you threw the first punch."

"Nobody's throwing punches here, you damn idiot. I didn't come to kick your ass, even if that is pretty fucking tempting. Are any of these kids students? Because you're supposed to register guests at the front desk." I glanced around.

"Fuck administration's rules," he spat. "They're the ones who got us into this mess."

"Then why the hell don't you go after them instead of after Sabine, who can't change the basic situation? You know, unlike the people running the school? Like we've been doing for weeks?" I couldn't believe this idiot.

"I don't believe you've done a damn thing," he started, then stiffened when I set my briefcase on the table in the center of the room and snapped it open.

"The suit is a matter of public record." I pulled out a copy of the brief and slid it across toward him. "Here's a copy."

"I..." He hesitated, then scooped up the papers and glanced through them. "The hearing isn't even happening until next month!"

"That's the legal system for you. That's what has to happen if you take the high road. That's exactly what we're—"

"That's not good enough!" he screamed, weakly flinging the papers in my general direction. They flapped to the table and the floor chaotically, none of them landing near me. "I want her out now. Now. Get the cunt out now."

"My God, do you need psychological help," I groaned. "This is not how life as an adult works."

I heard a noise behind me and felt someone coming up in my blind spot. I snapped my briefcase closed and, purely on reflex, spun around and brought it up, just in time to block the chair one of his fuckboy followers was swinging at me.

The impact sent a shock up my arm and broke the cheap wood in two places. He tried to swing it again, and I stepped forward, slamming the corner of the briefcase under his jaw. "Call off your dogs, Carmody!" I warned, but it was too late.

These little shits had come here spoiling for a beatdown and were ready to jump anyone their piece-of-shit leader pointed them at. Maybe they were too young for regular jail and figured why not. Or maybe they really were that dumb.

The three who tried to jump me first went down, one unconscious under a broken chair, one bleeding from his nose and sobbing on his knees, and one holding his balls and retching. I didn't give a shit. They kept coming, and I kept striking back.

Carmody's smirk slowly dissolved. His eyes looked worried as I shoved my way toward him, shaking loose two of his goons as I went. Blows rained down on my back and arms as I moved toward him, determined to pin him down for security. I was sure as hell that someone must have overheard the fight and called them by now.

"Get him!" one of his idiot followers yelled.

Another barked, "Ow, fuck. He hit me in the mouth!"

And another one staggered back bleeding, tears brimming in his eyes.

For once, I was glad my father had stuck me in self-defense classes since I was tiny. But even that couldn't help me if they piled on, and they just kept coming as I knocked them back and tried to get across the room. Maybe I should have focused on not getting hit, but I was too pissed off at that smug prick on the couch.

There were too many. I fought them off as long as I kept my feet, but some of them were swinging chairs. When the second one broke across my back, I went down, and they started kicking.

"Get that cuck! Kick his ass!" Their yells all blended together after a while. I grabbed one of them and yanked his legs out from under him, bringing him down to my level and disabling him with a gut punch. I used him as a meat shield against some boot party as I tried to crawl under the table.

Then the far hallway door exploded open. "What the fuck is going on in here?" the floor monitor bellowed. "Security is on its way!"

The boys stampeded instantly, pouring toward the closer door in a panic and flattening me as they ran over me. Carmody went whimpering and panting by, total panic in his voice, as if he had just now realized you couldn't orchestrate a beatdown in a dorm common room without being caught.

"Carmody!" the monitor yelled, making the bastard whimper harder as he tried to push himself faster than a jog. "I saw your face, you fucking loser. You're going to answer for this."

He followed them out as I lay there catching my breath. I was sore and bloodied, but nothing broken, and Carmody had just fucked himself. As I dragged myself to a sitting position, I saw the mess his cronies had made of the room and smiled grimly around a cut lip. It was only a matter of time now before he went down.

But that wasn't soon enough. Time had proven that when you squeezed Carmody, more and more crazy started leaking out. And he was about to get squeezed damn hard. Until he was safely behind bars, he was a hazard to Sabine.

Grabbing my briefcase and checking around for anything else I'd left, I pulled myself to my feet then picked up all of the lawsuit papers, shoving them back into my briefcase. I could hear yelling from down the hall. At least one of the unfamiliar petty thugs had gotten himself collared. Too bad it wasn't Carmody himself.

Wiping blood off my lip, I walked out through the far exit, making myself scarce before the monitor could catch and detain me. I needed to get to Sabine as fast as I could.

CHAPTER 19

SABINE

IT WAS ALMOST ten at night, and I was in the middle of editing an article for my blog. I heard a soft knock at the door, followed by a faint thud and a sigh. "Sabine?" Marcus called out, sounding exhausted.

Immediately worried, I got up and walked over to the door. "Yeah, just give me a minute."

I opened the door—and stared in shock as Marcus nearly fell inside, battered. His shirt was torn, his dark hair askew, and his knuckles bloodied. "Hi," he said with an awkward smile as he leaned heavily on the doorframe. "I was in the neighborhood, thought I'd visit."

"What the hell happened?" I helped him inside and over to the edge of my bed, where he flopped down heavily. I locked the door and turned back to eye him.

"Negotiations with Carmody and his cronies didn't go so well," he sighed, his smile tight and embarrassment in his eyes. "I'm not bad in a fight, but it was nine-on-one, and a couple guys tried to brain me with a chair."

"Jesus." I grabbed my first aid kit from my closet and

brought it over along with a packet of baby wipes. "You okay? Let's get you cleaned up."

"I'll be fine," he grumbled, trying to fend me off as I helped him out of his jacket. He had some ugly welts across the side of his face and the back of his neck, and one of his eyes was slightly swollen. "Okay, come on, you don't have to fuss."

"Yeah, I do. You're beaten up because of me." It came out before I even thought about it.

He eyed me tiredly. "No, I'm in this condition because of Carmody and his little hate cult of shit-disturbers. They're the ones who smashed a chair over my back and then kicked me in my ribs."

"We should call the police, or at least campus security." I was getting sick of the Gentlemen's refusal to get the police involved. I knew they were trying to save the reputations of both their fraternity and their campus, but it just wasn't worth it. What was the point of keeping quiet about these incidents if people kept getting hurt?

"No," he sighed, and he smirked when I rolled my eyes in exasperation. "I'll heal. As for Carmody and the others, they'll face consequences, all right. Security already knows about the wrecked common room and about Carmody's involvement. Unless he recruited from off campus, the other guys will eventually get caught. And he and the others will face consequences from Alpha Omega too. We will ban anyone involved from pledging again. It'll make Carmody go nuclear, but that just means a phone call from his mommy. Who will be very interested to know he's been inciting riots on campus."

My eyebrows rose. "You're going to sic his mother on him?"

He grinned. "Let's put it this way. His daddy is always off on business trips, which makes Carmody his mother's responsibility. From what I've heard, he treats her as badly as any other woman who crosses his path—but she just takes it. Spoils him.

Once she finds out he's damaging the school's reputation with his behavior and we're on the brink of having him arrested, she'll probably pull her precious baby out altogether to keep him from getting himself in worse trouble."

"What she needs to do is cut off his money until he gets his unwashed ass into therapy," I sighed as I started cleaning the blood and grime off his face.

He squinted and squirmed a little. "Come on, that's unnecessary."

"Let me fuss," I insisted, and he finally gave in and let me tend to him. "How is your head?"

"Good. I've always had a thick skull." His pupils were the same size, at least. "Have they been harassing you?"

"Nasty emails and hang-up calls, mostly. I can handle it. Carmody's got to go, though. Now that he's being kicked out of any connection to the fraternity, what happens if he does anything else? He doesn't seem to care or think about consequences, and when they arrive, they just make him crazier."

"Depends on what he does. But we're already gathering evidence, and Blake has spoken to his lawyer in case Carmody's parents complain about our refusal to let him pledge again for the umpteenth year." He winced as I cleaned a cut above his eyebrow. "Ow."

"You're going to have some nasty bumps and bruises. I still can't believe those bastards did this. This is some criminal bullshit."

"Yeah, tell me about it," he grumbled quietly as I finished cleaning his face and neck and opened up the kit. "Let me do the disinfecting," he demanded as I pulled out the antibiotic ointment.

I hesitated, then gave up the tube. "Okay. What do I do now?"

"I came over here because it was closer than the frat house, and because I wanted to make sure those fuckers didn't come trooping over here while they were all riled up." He touched the back of my hand briefly. "They put one bruise on you, and I'd have to kill them."

He took off his torn shirt, and I checked his back, seeing several more welts but no more broken skin. "Do your ribs hurt?"

"They're not cracked or anything. I'm just beaten up and tired." He examined the badly ripped shirt, missing several of its buttons. "What the hell is wrong with those guys?"

"Isn't it obvious?" I sighed as I tried not to stare at his muscular back. Marcus spent a lot of time being a charming goofball and one voice of reason among the Gentlemen. He also usually dressed pretty nicely, and unlike his cousin, he was neither imposingly tall nor particularly broad. But under his shirt, he had the body of a swimmer. "They hate women. They also hate any men who are at all successful with women."

"Short form, they hate anyone who isn't them." He smirked, but his eyes stayed dull. "How the hell did a bunch of misanthropic fuckups get in here? They're way more trouble than you ever were."

It was gratifying to hear him say that out loud finally, though he had seemed to think it all along. "Their parents' money, remember?"

"Christ. Yeah, I know too many of us from rich families to disagree with you about how that spoils people. You know I pledged alongside Carmody three years ago? He was a weaselly little loser then, and he sure is now. I don't even think getting laid would help his personality any." He rubbed his bruised jawline, then went back to dabbing ointment on his cuts and scrapes.

"Nobody wants to take one for the team for some asshole who hates women anyway." I gently smoothed his hair.

"Besides, most of us are busy with guys who deserve our attention."

He smiled up at me wistfully. "You know, when I found out about you and Nathaniel, I got kind of jealous."

"Well, I don't see why," I replied gently, taking the ointment when he was done, putting the cap on it. "I'm not doing anything to make you jealous. If you guys are having issues with one another, it's not because I'm trying to cause you problems."

He leaned into my hand a little. "Yeah, I guess we were the ones who were trying to play mind games. I'm sorry about that."

"Well, just as long as it doesn't happen again," I chided gently.

"I don't want to drive you away," he sighed. "I hope the bruises prove whose side I'm on."

"They do pretty well. I want to kill that bastard Carmody. Do you really think his mother will do anything about him?" I couldn't control my anger at Carmody right then, not with Marcus still tending fresh wounds. "The prick needs a cage. As long as he's running around free on campus, I don't feel safe."

Marcus nodded slowly, frowning. "I understand. I wouldn't either in your shoes. How about we take turns keeping you company here until this blows over?"

I tilted my head, considering, then smirked. "That would mean spending the night with me. You got an ulterior motive or what?"

He laughed, then winced. "Ow. Okay, maybe my ribs are a little sore. As for the answer to your question, I do. But that's not the point. Well, not all the point."

He managed a shit-eating grin despite his pain, and I had to laugh. "Well, if you can think about sex after being beat up, I'm guessing you're fine."

"Sweetheart, with you around, I could think about sex during open heart surgery." He almost sounded serious.

"Well, don't do that. You'll make the attending think you've got the world's weirdest fetish." I sat down next to him, setting aside the first aid kit. "I'm just glad you weren't hurt worse."

He slipped a warm arm around me, and I felt an answering surge of heat that surprised me. "Me too. I couldn't take advantage of being here if I was too high on the injured list."

He slid his hand up and down my back, leaving a tingling trail behind, and I blinked in surprise as I felt the mood turning fast. "Wow. Um, you sure you're up to this?" I was kind of hoping he'd say yes, but some of those welts were nasty.

He stared at me, then scoffed and pulled me in for an intense kiss.

I let out a soft whimper and returned it, quietly delighted. Of all the men aiming to be my new lovers, Marcus was the one I thought I could be friends with the most. I hadn't realized just how attracted I was to him until he finally touched me.

His kiss was more lingering and tender than those of his companions. He seemed to want to savor me. His mouth tasted like mint gum and coffee, and his tongue teased into my mouth so nimbly that he was stimulating the insides of my lips with it before I knew he had done it.

I barely noticed when he pulled me onto his lap, the kiss was so intense. I was there, arms and legs wrapping around him to steady myself as he drew me close. "Holy crap," he breathed as the kiss finally broke. "I've been wanting to do that for weeks."

That made me smile against his mouth. "Yeah?"

"Yeah." His dark eyes sparkled with desire.

"Which part? The kiss? Or having me on your lap? Or grabbing my ass?" He had me by both cheeks, kneading me through my jeans.

"Uh, yes?" he managed before leaning in for another kiss. I laughed, and then he silenced me with his mouth.

I hadn't lingered like this with the other two, just kissing and exploring each other with our hands. It made me feel like I was back in high school, hopelessly horny but holding back as much as I could, not wanting the moment to end. Marcus felt good against me, from his minty mouth to the bay rum aftershave to the slight sweat from his fight. I skimmed my fingers over his bare torso, along his shoulders, down his arms, avoiding his wounds. Sometimes I used my nails, running them delicately against his skin and making him shiver.

His slowness stoked the hunger in me, making me impatient, and my impatience made me bold. Eagerly, I pulled off my sweater, leaving me sitting on his lap in my camisole and bra. He pulled back and stared at me delightedly, then helped me tug off the camisole. He cupped my breasts reverently, started nibbling on them lightly through the bra, teasing me until I shivered and made little sounds of delight.

He teased me for a long time, kissing around the bra instead of removing it, while I whimpered and panted and finally gave up and undid the clasp between my breasts. Even then, he only kissed me softly, covering every inch of my skin with tender brushes of his lips while ignoring my nipples standing painfully in the cool air.

"Tease," I groaned as he unbuckled my belt and then his own. My back arched as he ran his hands down my back. His breath blew over my sensitive skin, but he still didn't suckle me.

His eyes danced with mischief. "Hey, I waited a while for this." He reached into his pocket and pulled out a condom. "You can handle a little teasing."

He nuzzled between my breasts as I sat up enough to unzip his fly. "Not too much," I purred, but he smirked and kept right on pretending my aching nipples didn't exist. "One second." I stood, sliding out of my jeans and panties.

He kicked off his shoes and socks and yanked his trousers down. I saw a few more welts on his legs and squashed a surge of rage and remorse. Now wasn't time to talk about what had happened. Now was the time to get our minds off it.

I blinked when I saw his throbbing cock, which was as big around as my wrist. My eyes widened slightly. "Damn, boy."

He laughed and tore the condom packet open. "Oh, don't worry," he responded with a sly little grin as I helped him roll the latex onto his monster. "It'll fit fine once I get you wet enough."

When he sat down, I decided two things. I was going to test his theory for as long as I could stand it—and I would not let Blake know there was someone in the pack who was hung bigger than him.

"Kneel up over me again," he instructed, and I did as he leaned back, propping himself against the window. He gripped my hips in his hands, slid them over my bare ass, then glided them up my sides to cup my breasts again. When he finally sucked my nipple into his mouth, I had to grit my teeth against a scream.

His fiery mouth tugged at me firmly while I rocked against him, brushing his throbbing cock with the lips of my pussy. Every time I did, I felt him shiver slightly. I felt him slide the head across my pussy, which was already wet with anticipation. But then he held it there, neither pulling me down nor thrusting upward.

Instead, he propped his knuckle against my clit, pressing gently as his mouth teased and nibbled at my nipples. I moaned and circled my hips, feeling him slide deeper with each slow grind. His dark eyes closed, lips parted and trembling as he fought the urge to push into me.

His slow, almost tender teasing drove me wild. I panted, grinding faster as he stroked me slowly, our bodies joined, his cock sliding in a half inch at a time as I shimmied my hips. He filled me, stretching me a little, the intensity enhancing the rising pleasure mounting in my groin as he caressed my clit.

Finally, I couldn't stand it, and I bored down on him, taking the rest of him in as he jerked his head back and panted hoarsely. His cock rubbed me in places I hadn't stimulated before. I whimpered around a bitten lip as he stroked me, holding still inside me.

I bounced my hips over him, circling them faster and faster as I felt my body ramp up toward orgasm. I was on top, but he was the one in control, teeth at my neck and fingers teasing me until I shook and twisted around him in an involuntary dance. His eyes fluttered closed, but then he slowed, and I slowed too, retreating from climax and staying in the frantic, trembling, tingling delight just before. "Easy, baby," he rasped, chest heaving. "Not yet."

We rode together like that, pleasure rising toward completion and then ebbing back again as he backed off to keep from finishing, repeatedly. My pussy was tight around him, the slight frustration of holding off nothing in the face of anticipation. He wasn't like Blake, just slightly cruel. Marcus only wanted it to last and last, until neither of us could stand it anymore.

Finally, we were both too keyed up to back off again. I dug my nails into his shoulders, and he dug his fingers into my hips, kissing me hungrily as we moaned into each other's mouths. We ground together, muscles taut, and I felt him go rigid under me a second before I came.

The climax rocked me so hard that I broke the kiss and screamed into his shoulder, barely aware enough to muffle the sound. He didn't care. His shouts of bliss practically rattled the windows.

When I came back to myself, he was panting against my shoulder, that enormous tool still shaking a little inside me. I clung to him, and we held each other until, finally, I felt his erection dwindle inside me. "Can you get up?" he asked hoarsely. "I've got to get rid of this thing."

He grabbed the base of the condom, and I stood up, legs rubbery but holding me up as he slid out from under me. Barely awake and suddenly cold, I slid under the comforter and lay there with my heart slowing as I heard him finish up in the bathroom and come back out.

His belt buckle rattled as he retrieved his boxers. I glanced back and saw him step and tuck into them, his dark eyes hooded with contentment. I rolled back over, and he slid into bed behind me, spooning me and kissing my neck. "Holy shit, that was worth the wait," he purred.

I smiled contentedly. "Yeah."

As I drifted off, I stared through the slats of my blinds and saw someone standing down in the parking lot. I caught the pale half oval of a bearded face tilted up at us and wondered why someone was standing in a snowstorm. No way had whoever it was heard Marcus all the way out in the parking lot. But they just kept standing there until I finally lost interest and let my eyes fall closed.

CHAPTER 20

SABINE

THE NEXT DAY, Daniel took a shift as my night's bodyguard. He insisted on taking me out to dinner before we settled in for the night. I supposed he considered it gentlemanly, but with everything that was going on, I would have preferred to order in a pizza and eat in the warm, familiar sanctum of my dorm room.

"Have you thought about what you will tell your mother about the lot of us?" he asked me gently as I carefully sipped a glass of white wine. The slab of salmon on the plate in front of me was about twice what I could eat, but Daniel was tearing into his fish like he hadn't eaten in a week.

I laughed in embarrassment and quieted it with a sip of my wine. "Um. No? I would be shy about telling her about one boyfriend. I can only imagine what she's going to think about how things are developing between us."

It wasn't a formal agreement. They had agreed to court me without jealousy, but I was setting the pace here, and I was feeling things out as I went along. I knew from my reading that polyamory could get complicated fast, especially without enough communication. It intimidated me, but I couldn't choose between the four guys I had dated so far, and I didn't want to.

Daniel's smile went a little mischievous. "I suppose that is understandable," he purred. "Though I hope you're not ashamed of us."

"No." It was more a fear of Mom judging me, not them. "I'm not ashamed of you. I'm just still getting used to all of this myself. I haven't even figured out how to explain to her I'm not a virgin anymore."

That really was going to take some explaining. Mom was Catholic, but she was also very practical, and she had been to college herself. She knew that even if sex wasn't inevitable, exploration of it was. But we had never had that talk once I had qualified to come here for college. Not much of one anyway. She had been too worried about guys like Carmody to even talk to me about guys like Daniel.

"Is it necessary to tell her? I lost mine years ago, and I never announced the matter to my parents at all." He bit another chunk of salmon off his fork.

"I don't have to tell her. But eventually, we have to figure something out. If more than one guy comes to visit me over summer break, and you all seem to know one another, she's going to have questions." I smiled at him wryly as his amber eyes danced. "Any pointers?"

"Well, we'll just have to impress her and be very respectful, then. The burden shouldn't just be on you." He winked, and I relaxed a little. "But I seriously doubt any of us will want to back down on the time we spend with you so you can pretend to be monogamous."

"I wouldn't do that to any of you," I protested.

He smiled and nodded. "No. I didn't mean to imply that. You seem rather open-minded for someone with so little dating experience." His smile went lopsided again as I glanced away shyly. "I meant it as a compliment."

"Well," I admitted, "at least it meant that I didn't have to choose between any of you."

"No, you didn't. And I'm glad of that. I fear that if we had had to fight over you, it might have torn us apart as friends." He gazed at me hungrily. "I know I would never have backed down."

I laughed. "You wouldn't?"

"Never. Believe me, I could stand up to even Blake with ease. Or Blake and Marcus." He seemed to consider how such a fight would go for a moment. "I wouldn't want to do it, though."

"It shouldn't be necessary." I took a few bites of my salmon, then realized Daniel had gone quiet.

I glanced up and saw him staring over my shoulder at someone, his smile gone. He muttered something in German, sounding annoyed.

"What is it?" I asked.

"Carmody."

"You have got to be kidding me," I growled, turning around. I wasn't afraid, even after everything. No matter what he had stirred up the campus idiots to do, Carmody had never had the balls to confront me directly without a crowd at his back. *No. I was pissed.* "He's stalking me now? Against the damned protection order? I thought his mommy would have pulled him out of school."

"According to Blake, she hasn't been answering her phone," Daniel sighed as I stared at Carmody. His eyes avoided mine as he squirmed in his seat instead, his battered, wet trilby pulled down over his eyes.

"I'm calling him out," I growled, getting up. I knew he had received notice of the emergency protection order I had filed, and here he was, violating it already. Daniel immediately stood to back me up, and we walked right over to Carmody's table.

He immediately got up and hurried out so fast that he knocked over his chair. I whipped out my phone and took a photo of him fleeing. "He just violated the protection order."

"That would explain his fleeing. But I find it rather interesting that he will only confront you as part of a group or through proxies." Daniel pulled out my chair for me at our table, and we sat back down. "He almost seems frightened of you."

"He's chickenshit," I muttered, stabbing at my salmon with a fork. "Marcus said Carmody didn't lift a finger during the beating, just had the other guys do it while he stood back and watched."

"Yes, and now Carmody is on the hook for both the disturbance and the mess. If you report the protection order violation, he'll be in even worse trouble. Which I would love to see right about now." Daniel didn't discourage me, which surprised me. Instead, he was disgusted as I felt.

"Yeah, that's what the protection order's there for." I was perversely excited at the prospect of seeing Carmody led away in handcuffs. Blake had set so many conditions on my getting the police involved that I was resenting it—especially after Marcus had gotten hurt. "I just don't understand why he's acting even worse after the order came down and his actions got him banned from pledging again."

"Like many cowardly men, he blames the nearest convenient woman for his problems." Daniel swirled his wine in his glass and then took a sip. "You know, if it makes things easier on you, I'm happy to bite the bullet and help you explain things to your mother."

"You are?" I smiled with relief, instantly distracted from my simmering resentment. "Thank you. I didn't really know how to ask anyone."

"We'll need a plan. Fortunately, it's a good while before summer break."

We talked about it through the rest of dinner and on the way back. There was no sign of Carmody in the parking lot. "Thanks for staying with me tonight," I said as we rode the elevator upstairs.

"My pleasure. So, what are you putting on your blog about Carmody's stalking?" Daniel didn't sound concerned about it. Blake's controlling streak was sexy as hell in bed, but I kept having to push back against it when it came to Carmody. Hopefully cutting ties between him and the fraternity would help keep the frat's nose clean once Carmody's jailing made the news.

"The truth. Well, the parts I feel like sharing. He's stalking me, I'm having friends stay with me at night in case he violates his protection order again, and I'm calling the cops about the violation and sending them the photo. Which I will also post online." It was a great photo. Carmody running out with a panicked look on his face, holding his battered hat, trench coat flapping behind him.

Daniel chuckled. "I want to watch you put this together. Are you doing a video as well?"

My smile faded as we stepped out of the elevator on my floor. "No. I've been too busy." Literally getting busy. At this point, I had gotten laid—and gotten deep, proper sleep—so much that schoolwork felt like a breeze and Carmody felt like trivia, but I was flaking off on some of my responsibilities. "Still, I have the best excuse possible."

That made him laugh as he followed me down the hall. "Are we making life harder on you?"

"Not really. But I do sometimes wonder how I'm going to keep up with all of you." Though, if that turned out to be the biggest problem in our complicated relationship, I knew I would be lucky.

"Just trust us. We're supposed to be taking care of one another, not just you taking care of us. If you're getting worn out, we're not treating you right." He stood by as I unlocked my dorm room door, then followed me in, glancing around. "Not the largest, but it's lovely. Especially given that it does double duty as your broadcast studio."

"Yeah, well, I've done well with less for most of my life," I acknowledged without resentment, only amusement that it surprised him.

"We need to get you into your own apartment. I'd suggest moving you in to the fraternity house, but…"

"But that's for fraternity members," I finished for him as I took off my coat and hung it up in my closet. "I'm fine here. I don't want to spend money on rent when I can have a room and my own bathroom that the scholarship covers."

He pulled a face, and I snorted and shook my head as I took his coat and hung it up too. "You deserve better."

"There are a ton of people out there who deserve better than they get, Daniel. And many who get better than they deserve." Like Carmody, for example. "I'm fine here for now."

"Just thinking it might be better if Carmody couldn't find you so easily." He winced as he settled into the one chair, and I perched on the edge of my bed. He didn't make a move toward me, content just to talk for now.

"Hiding from him isn't the answer. He won't stop, even if he doesn't have the balls to face me directly. He needs to be in jail. He violated the protection order by stalking me. I have evidence on my phone. I should make the call now."

He didn't stop me as I called the police and reported the

violation. I forwarded them the photograph and received a promise that they would enter it into evidence and that they would send a car to pick Carmody up. It took all of fifteen minutes, but by the end of that time, I felt drained.

"That's it," I sighed, rubbing my temple. Daniel moved over onto the bed, appearing concerned as he reached for me.

Outside, something slammed against the window below ours. I heard an astonished curse from my downstairs neighbor and turned to the window, peering out through the slats of the blinds just as orange light bloomed from below. Daniel leaned over beside me to check.

A small crowd with something that looked like a very large slingshot was standing on the strip of lawn between the sidewalk and the parking lot. The slingshot was stuck into it and leaned far back, while two of the guys pulled the strap back and another grabbed one bottle from a small cluster of them and lit the rag hanging from its neck.

The bushes at the base of my column of windows were on fire, the falling snow keeping the flaming patch from spreading. "You got to be fucking kidding me," I breathed.

I felt the bed shift next to me—and a second later, my dorm door slammed shut. I rolled over. Daniel had left without his coat.

My downstairs neighbor was at his window, screaming out at the maniacs slinging Molotov cocktails at us. "What the fuck are you assholes doing? I'm calling campus security."

They let another one fly. It arced toward my window—and a gust of wind smashed it against the stucco-coated cinder block beside the glass. The burning alcohol drizzled down, sizzling as the snow hit it, leaving nothing behind but a scorch mark.

These bastards are insane. I grabbed my phone and camera and dialed 9-1-1 while I filmed.

I had barely gotten the number dialed in when I saw

Daniel sprint out toward the group and run full tilt into the guy holding the Molotov.

The burning bottle dropped into the others, and they went up, sending the guys operating the slingshot scattering and setting it on fire. Daniel started beating the boy down hard, ignoring the flames almost at his feet, while I stared in astonishment. I could hear his furious German four stories up.

The other guys tried to pull Daniel off him, while from a nearby car, I saw Carmody hurrying forward, flailing his arms and yelling at them. Then he saw something at the far end of the lot and ran for it, lumbering back between the cars and vanishing as the others scattered like frightened rats. The one in Daniel's grip twisted free and stumbled off, holding his nose, leaving dark splotches on the snow behind him.

Daniel turned and stalked back inside. Several seconds later, a campus security cruiser rolled to a stop next to the burning slingshot. The guy who got out was yelling into his walkie-talkie as he ran around to grab a fire extinguisher from his trunk.

I started shaking, only then realizing just how scared I had been. When I heard a knock at the door, I got up and raced for it.

Daniel stood on the other side, broad chest heaving, snowflakes still caught in his spiky hair. He stepped inside, and I threw myself into his arms as soon as he shut the door behind himself. "I can't believe you did that. Are you all right?" I gasped into his neck.

He pulled me closer against him, his heart beating fast. "Yes, I'm fine. Just cold. I saw what they were trying to do to your dorm room and just lost my temper." One big, square hand circled the back of my neck. His fingers were icy, but I felt the caress down to my toes.

"Thank you," I whispered against his skin and felt the jolt go through him.

"Hold that thought," he murmured into my hair. "I imagine campus security will need to speak with us."

They did. My heart was pounding so hard it made me dizzy. The interview raced past, and I didn't even remember what the security officer looked like afterward. I forwarded a copy of the film to them—after cutting out the part where Daniel ran out to whip ass. I didn't want them picking him up on assault charges.

Finally, they left us alone, and I stood shivering in the middle of my room, wondering if I should check in to a hotel. "They tried to set me on fire, and my whole dorm room with me," I gasped as Daniel moved up behind me.

"They failed miserably," he murmured in my ear, his hands settling on my shoulders.

"Maybe I should leave here." I wrapped my arms around myself. "Maybe I should hide."

He covered my arms with his and kissed the back of my neck. "No. You're right. You can't let them scare you into running. They'll see it as a win. The police are searching for them now. Let them be the ones who face consequences."

I turned around. "But..."

He laid a finger over my lips, then slid his arms around me again. "No. Stay here. Stay with me and don't be afraid. I—we —won't let them hurt you. Ever."

I protested, the fear those flames had stoked still boiling in me—but then suddenly, Daniel's mouth covered mine, muffling me. His firm, commanding kiss took my breath away and distracted me from my terror at once.

I gasped through my nose, shocked by the sheer power of my body's response, and wrapped my arms around him. I slid my hands over his back, tracing the bunched, steely muscles, feeling them relax slowly under my touch. His rage was fading, but even before it had, it didn't scare me. I still wasn't used to men being angry on my behalf, rage aimed at protecting me. There was something sexy about that.

I moaned into his mouth, and he kissed me harder, almost bruising, pushing me back against the wall and sandwiching me firmly between it and his body. He burrowed his thigh in between mine and lifted, leaving me on my toes, straddling it as I braced against the wall. When he broke the kiss, his eyes were glazed with lust.

"Let me take your mind off everything," he murmured against my mouth.

"You already have, with that kiss," I gasped.

He chuckled. "I'm only getting started." And his mouth covered mine again.

His impatient lust caught me up in it fast. We ended up tangled up together against the wall, hands burrowing into gaps in clothing, unbuttoning, unzipping, pulling shirts up hurriedly, covering freshly bared skin with kisses and marks from teeth. His skin tasted faintly of salt and smoke, and his muscles jerked when I ran my tongue over his belly.

It took almost nothing to ready me for him, but despite all the half-clothed clawing at each other, he took his time. Our frenzy broke up into individual moments that caught in my memory. Me pressed against the wall, breasts tingling under his fingers as he ran his tongue up my spine. Me rolling my head back and forth as he held me up, legs around his waist as he sucked my nipples until they almost hurt. His teeth grazing my hip. The trail of hickeys he left down my belly while I leaned on the wall, legs trembling.

He stopped to roll on the condom then held me up against

the wall as he entered me, hands under my ass, lifting me as if I weighed nothing. I clung to him with arms and legs as he thrust in, his head falling back with a jerk and a shuddering groan coming from us both. His belly flexed as he ground his hips against me, shivering violently every time he pushed in, his breathing harsh in my ear.

He was like a machine, moving hard against me, the slap of our hips together driving my pleasure upward little by little as he struggled harder and harder not to come inside me. His powerful muscles were taut with pleasure, his fingers digging into my ass cheeks firmly, and every time our bellies smacked together, his soft grunts got a little more desperate.

We didn't even have all our clothes properly off by the time he sank to his knees with me propped over them, holding me by the hips as he pushed up into me. I barely noticed my bra still hanging around my neck or my socks still on. Barely noticed my nails digging into his shoulders. I squirmed, teased up to the edge of orgasm, and he let go with one hand to press its heel into the top of my pussy as he bounced me up against it.

I squealed with delight, riding up over the edge in seconds, and dug my knees into the thin carpeting as I rocked against him in time to my spasms. He didn't cry out as he came, instead hissing through his teeth and arching up into me in one long, powerful stroke. He shuddered, trembling, and then sank down, head fallen back and grip loosening as he let out a sigh of contentment.

I came down from my climax trembling and limp, my head propped on his shoulder as we caught our breath. I was too wobbly to stand, so after a minute, he slipped out of me and scooped me up, carrying me to the bed. I got my bra off, tossing it away, and then he was tucking me in at the outer edge and going off to rid himself of the condom.

I dozed. When I came back to myself, he was lying between me and the chilly window, shielding me from the slight draft. He was quiet, his back to me. His breathing was slow but not deep. He was awake and keeping watch, just in case. A sense of comfort filled me, and I drifted into sleep.

CHAPTER 21

SABINE

DANIEL LEFT me to go to his early morning gym class before dawn had fully broken. I felt safe enough by then to let him go without protest. I knew campus security had picked up Carmody and his people before the night was over, and that meant Carmody would now be in the hands of the police. Attempted arson was a serious charge. So was attempted murder. If his mother really was out of town, there would be no one around to pay his bail.

Maybe I would get lucky and never see his ugly face again.

Yawning and exhausted, I was just a little sore from my acrobatic sex with Daniel. Thinking back over the four encounters I'd had with four very different men, I honestly couldn't decide which I had liked better.

Nathaniel's surprise passion had helped me give up control.

Blake's intensity and control of my orgasm had left me craving more.

Marcus's tenderness and patience had left me in a frenzy.

Daniel's athleticism and sheer power had left me

wondering what other positions he could twist me into and make me like it. Against the wall. On the floor. Braced against the bed and on top of it. We had all thoroughly christened this dorm room. I wondered what would happen if we had an entire house to use. *Where else would we end up? Kitchen table? On top of the washer? Bathtub?* No way of knowing.

Whatever else was happening, as long as I stayed with these guys, I knew my sex life was going to be anything but boring.

I sat up, yawning and stretching, feeling little twinges from the finger-bruises on my back. I could still remember his hoarse groans in my ear, as I slid from beneath the comforter and headed into my bathroom for a shower. I didn't really want to wash his musky scent off me, but I was itchy from dried sweat and my muscles needed soothing water.

Showered off, I dressed, settling into my seat at my computer to check my email and start working on my next post. I stifled a yawn as I logged in—and immediately froze.

A badly photoshopped porn image had replaced my latest post, with my face in place of the woman's and Carmody's face, the man's. The caption, "I'm a stupid whore lol," was in red beneath it.

I immediately changed my password to a thirty-character randomized one and switched out the post, then checked again. No other alterations. Carmody had only started fucking around with my blog, apparently. It must have taken a lot of work to crack my password, and I suspected he would crack this one eventually too.

He had sent me an email as well.

You fucking whore, you had me thrown in jail.

I had to have my mother pay bail. How fucking dare you!

I'm going to rape your school records.

I'm going to rape your precious blog, your bank accounts... everything, bitch!

I'll destroy your whole life without leaving my desk.

Heart pounding with outrage, I changed all my passwords to more elaborate ones and then called Blake.

"Did you miss your ride to breakfast?" he yawned in my ear. "I can send someone over."

"No. Carmody got out of jail and has started on a hacking attack. I need help. It's only a matter of time before he breaks in to my accounts again. And he's threatening my school records." Somehow, I kept my voice calm.

Blake was silent for a long moment, then sighed. "I'll send our computer expert over while we search for him. If anything else happens, call me at once."

"I will. Thank you." I hung up and started working on a fresh blog post, giving a recap of everything Carmody had done to me that semester, the protection order, his violating the protection order, how Alpha Omega had kicked him out, his attempt to use a bunch of stupid freshmen to help him set my dorm room on fire, and how the moment his mommy paid his bail, he turned around, threatened me, hacked my blog and posted porn on it, and was trying to do worse.

I was adding a copy of the email and a cropped image of his smug face from the porn photo when I heard a sharp knock at the door. I got up at once, searching around for a weapon and then balled up my fist. "Who is it?"

"It's Jude. Don't be angry. I'm the team programmer." He sounded just a touch guarded, as if he was expecting a punch in the nose when I opened the door.

He didn't get one. I let him in and gestured to the desk. "Thanks for coming."

He hurried past me, blond hair askew and eyes sleepy.

"Give campus security a call and send them his threats. Meanwhile, I'll take care of the rest."

"Got it." I sat down on the bed and got to work as he slid into my computer chair and pulled a high-end laptop out of his messenger bag. He plugged it in, got my Wi-Fi password, and started typing rapidly.

I called my bank first and instructed them not to accept any log-ins or attempts at password changes until I called them back. Same with my donation account. I called campus security and campus IT about the problem and dealt with a million questions and two sets of likely empty promises. That done, I checked on Jude.

"What are you up to?" I couldn't even recognize the lines of code flowing from his fingers. I had taken him for a typical jock, but here he was, coming out with the top-notch nerdery I would have expected from Nathaniel.

"Making a few minor adjustments to his account behind his back. Just making sure he ends up aimed at the wrong target while thinking he's putting you through hell."

I scooted to the edge of my bed and peered over his shoulder. "Wait. Who and how?"

"Basically, I'm hacking his attack programs and altering them as they go out. He'll see your bank account, your email account, and your blog, but he'll be attacking someone else's. Complete with draining accounts, doing password lockouts, and—" he peered at some code streaming past "—posting more photoshopped porn."

"Who is he doing it to? Himself?" I saw another email full of threats fill the screen for a few seconds. This time, he was threatening rape and mutilation. *What a classy guy.*

Jude smirked. "Nope. His mother."

I let out an incredulous laugh. "Oh my God. Well, I can't

say she doesn't deserve it after coddling him and refusing to listen to what he's been doing."

"That's it exactly." He smirked. "And she can't discount what he's doing if she thinks he's now doing it to her. Including draining her money."

I watched mutely as he waged a war based in code and deception, typing faster than I had ever seen, occasionally showing flashes of the garbage Carmody was unwittingly unloading on his own mother. "I'd give it another fifteen, twenty minutes before he has to log off thanks to the Wrath of Mom. Especially since he just zeroed out her bank account."

"He hasn't even noticed something weird about a college student's bank account being stuffed full of cash?" I didn't know how much Mrs. Carmody had left in her account after paying the little shit's bail, but it had to be a lot more than any broke scholarship student.

"Apparently, he's too worked up. That's the thing. The more pissed off he gets, the more mistakes he makes. That arson thing? That's a felony, and the parking lot security cameras caught him and the others at it. He's been trying to hurt you, but he's only damned himself. And he'll keep doing it until the moment it all comes crashing down on him." He smirked without looking up from his work.

"I just wish I could be there to see it," I sighed, vengeful glee replacing my outrage entirely. "I really appreciate this."

"Yeah, well, I appreciate the chance to make that dinner-party shit up to you. I haven't lived with myself very well since it happened." The amusement had left his voice. When he stared up at me, his eyes were full of regret. "I'm not Carmody. I grew out of that shit when I entered high school. Even pretending made me feel like shit. And I'm really fucking sorry."

I thought back to that night and how I had seethed as I had

walked back home—mostly because of him. Ultimately, they had all deceived me about who they were—and I would not forget it. Forgive, but not forget.

"This goes a long way toward making it up," I told him gently but firmly. "Ever start acting that way toward me again, though, and you'll regret it."

He cracked a grin. "Going to kick my ass?"

The corner of my mouth tugged up. "No, I'll just never let you touch me." Since I already knew he badly wanted to.

His smile faded a little. "Shit. Okay, that really is punishment. I'll mind my manners."

I laughed—and then blinked as one window on his screen went blank. "What happened?"

"He logged off." Jude scooted back in his chair. "Last thing he did was transfer the cash back into Mommy's account. My guess is, she's roasting his ass as we speak."

"Holy shit, you're a miracle worker." I kissed him impulsively—and he made a cheerful noise and grabbed the back of my neck to hold me and prolong the kiss.

"Wow," he muttered when we came up for air. He stood up, sending a quick text to someone—probably Blake—then shoved his phone back into the pocket of his leather jacket. "Any chance I can get another of those?"

I slipped into his arms, enjoying the scent of a different cologne, a different male musk under it. The bulge in his jeans pressed firmly against my belly, making all kinds of promises. *I think I'm about to miss my morning classes*, I thought feverishly as he lifted me half off my feet in his eagerness.

Jude's kiss was almost clumsy with sheer enthusiasm. He may not have been the oversexed idiot I expected from guys my same age, but only because the "idiot" part was missing. His mouth moved against mine so hungrily that I wondered if he had touched anyone in months. Or maybe he was just this shocked and gratified to have me in his arms after his one gigantic mistake.

"They're on their way over for a restaurant celebration. Blake's idea," he gasped against my mouth between kisses.

That barely gave us ten minutes. "We should probably—" I started, but he cut off the sentence with a rougher kiss that stole both my breath and my attention. His hand was already sliding up inside my shirt to cup my breast.

Before meeting the Gentlemen and having sex with each of them, I had never felt genuine sexual pleasure or desire in my life. Now, it was all I could feel. I ran my hands over him greedily, exploring a new body, while he grunted and jerked with pleasure, even more when I started using my nails.

I lost track of time. I didn't think ten minutes had passed yet, but suddenly, something heavy slammed hard against the door. It shook in its frame, and a photo of Mama's cabin next to it fell from the wall.

It happened again. *Bam.*

I broke the kiss, frowning in confusion. "The fuck are they doing? That isn't funny!" I raised my voice. "Hey, knock it off!"

Bam.

Jude grabbed my shoulder before I could go for the door. "It's not them."

"What?"

I heard heavy, throaty huffing outside and then a squealing grunt of effort a second before the heavy thud sounded again. "You whore!" came Carmody's hysterical yelling. "What did you do? My mother's cut me off. She's not paying for a lawyer this time. I'll kill you!"

I backed away from the door, bumping into Jude, who was texting again. "He's finally lost it," I breathed. "Where the hell are the cops?"

"Security's minutes away if someone's already called it in.

But our guys are already on their way. They'll drive him off." Jude didn't sound scared. He sounded pissed. "If I don't kick his ass for interrupting us!"

"Get in line," I demanded, just as furious, but for a million reasons besides that one. It sounded like Carmody was wearing himself out—and that was fine. When I got out there, his balls were going up between his teeth on the tip of my boot, and I didn't want to deal with grappling with his smelly ass first.

I heard Carmody's whining gasps for air. Then he shouted at someone, "Kick the door in!"

I froze as two smaller forms started pounding on the door instead. "Fuck, he's not alone."

Jude didn't even stop to say anything before shoving his body between me and the door. "Go hide in the bathroom, baby. I'll deal with them if they break through."

I hesitated before backing away as he walked up to the door. The pounding on the other side got louder and louder— and then suddenly, before I could even step into the bathroom, it stopped.

Shouting. A deep-voiced bellow. Someone swearing in German at the top of his lungs. Daniel had arrived. And that meant the others had too.

"Hey, ow!" yelled a strange guy's voice. "You don't have to grab me by the hair."

"We were just joking. We're just having fun. We didn't mean—ow! Stop hitting me." A thud, and the second stranger's voice went quiet.

The first one's voice went high with panic. "Okay, okay! I'm sorry! This wasn't even our idea."

"Get against the goddamned wall and wait for security," I heard Blake growl.

"No!" Carmody yelled, behaving like a gigantic baby. "No,

no, no! You can't let them win. This can't be allowed. That whore doesn't belong here."

I heard the sharp crack of a fist connecting—and then a thud. There was a loud sob—probably Carmody, because it sounded like a toddler whose tantrum had gotten him nowhere.

Jude unlocked the door and pulled it open to peer out at the aftermath of a four-on-four beatdown. Three guys I barely remembered from one of the many pranks and attacks stood back against the wall, staring nervously at Blake and the others, who were looming over them. And kneeling in the middle of the hallway, sweaty, red-faced, rumpled, his face wet with snot and tears, was Carmody, defeated.

He stared up at me with miserable little eyes. "You've ruined everything!" he sobbed.

"No," I argued, standing over him with my hands on my hips, ignoring that my shirt was untucked. "You have. Your actions fucked up your own life. You're just too much of a spoiled, irrational baby to take responsibility for it."

I heard running feet, and then four security officers and a cop were hurrying toward us. One of them exclaimed in astonishment as he saw Carmody. "This fucker again? Why isn't he still in jail?"

"Rich parents," the cop sighed. "His mommy posted bail in like ten minutes, so now here I am, picking him up again." He eyed me. "You okay?"

I nodded. "Yeah, my guys here handled it. Thanks for coming."

I turned a brilliant smile on my five boyfriends as they gathered around me protectively. The security guys and the cop looked a little confused as they gathered up the other assholes and then moved forward to drag Carmody to his feet.

Carmody blubbered as they put the cuffs on him. "We

should arrest her. She forced my hand. It's all her fault, not mine. Not mine! She's the one who doesn't belong here."

"I already told you," I informed him as he glared at me through a glaze of tears. "That's not your call. It's theirs." I glanced around at the Gentlemen. "And mine."

Carmody cried and whined all the way down the hall. I sighed, leaning against the wall. *It's done. It's over.*

Someone put a bottle of sports drink in my hand, and I took a grateful swallow. "I'm so glad you guys were here," I whispered. "Still got to figure out what I'm telling Mama about all this." *Maybe I would start with the rescue, and that I was okay.* But that would just open up a whole can of questions. All of which would need explanations.

"That's fine," Blake sighed, flicking lint off the sleeve of his immaculate jacket. "It comes with the territory now that you're ours."

"I just hope they have a good therapist at Rikers Island," I muttered as I watched them shove Carmody and the others into the elevator.

"They do." Marcus smirked. "It's called 'getting his ass kicked repeatedly by short-tempered cons until he grows up and learns to keep his damn mouth shut and stop being a giant pain in the ass.'"

"Good." I almost pitied the maladjusted bastard, now that it was over. But he would have killed me had he been able to get away with it, and God knew what else. And so my gratitude toward the Gentlemen went way beyond their making me feel safer. "You really think it's over now?" I murmured. I knew it had to be, but I still wanted the reassurance.

"Chances are, yes." Nathaniel moved past me to put my mom's photograph back up on its hook. "Once this story breaks wide, the cost of trying to harm you will be apparent to anyone left who might consider making trouble."

"Yeah, if there's even anyone left who does." Jude sounded confident. "Most of the guys on Carmody's little mailing list have already told him to fuck off and blocked him."

"And if they should try something," Daniel promised, nursing a few scrapes on his fist, "we'll be here."

"That makes me feel a lot better," I confided. "Let me get my coat." I kissed Jude on the cheek and murmured, "Rain check for tonight," in his ear. He grinned at me.

I was practically gloating while tucking in my shirt.

Fuck you, Carmody.

You lose.

I win.

We win.

"So, where are we going?" I asked, pulling on my coat. "I'm absolutely starved."

CHAPTER 22

SABINE

"WELL, everyone, I'm gearing up for my first round of college finals. And as I mentioned last time, the weather has been wild." I turned the camera out the window, tilting it down to show a parking lot blanketed with at least two feet of fresh powder. More was coming down.

"If this is any sign, the rest of winter is going to be wild too. But I'm doing just fine. I wanted to take this opportunity to thank you all for your support during this crazy semester. I didn't start this blog to showcase a lot of drama, but unfortunately, some guys around here turned out to be total drama queens. I'm happy to say that since the big mess two months ago, things have been nice and quiet. I've even been able to study in peace. What a difference multiple arrests make, huh?" I smiled.

"I can't talk much about the ongoing case against my stalker and his friends. But you'll be happy to know that he's awaiting trial without bail, and they have expelled the four guys who helped him try to burn down my dorm. Pretty much everyone else has moved on from giving me any problems. There is a lawsuit against the administration for deciding to make the school co-ed without providing the students with any official grievance process. Which I support, because say what you want about the need for more integrated campuses, it doesn't mean that the administration should get away with just ignoring student concerns like that." I paused. "Anyway, the lawsuit doesn't target me or my four-year scholarship. So next semester, I should be able to focus a lot more on my studies and the better parts of life here on campus. Those who have come here for the drama, I hope you won't be too disappointed." I winked. "But then again, I'll have two or three court cases to follow, both the campus lawsuit and the charges against Carmody. So hey, stay tuned!"

I turned off the camera, satisfied with the filmed introduction.

I didn't have time for much more before Blake picked me up for breakfast. I had been eating my meals over at the fraternity house even more now that Carmody and his people were no longer there.

My presence bothered no one at the house, nor did the fact that I was apparently dating one Gentleman. Sometimes I heard the other members or pledges guessing at which one. They didn't know it was all of them. I was still working out how to explain that to Mom. She knew that I was dating and that I was careful not to let it interfere with my studies. But she had no clue I was dating five men who all knew about one another.

It was a week before finals started, and I had absolutely nothing out of the ordinary to report on my blog. At least, nothing out of the ordinary that was anyone's business but mine.

The Gentlemen's lawsuit against the school was going to drag on for a long while, but that was fine. Half their reason for doing it was to shed light on poor administration-student relations, hoping to get the policies behind them changed. Whether the campus returned to being single-sex after I left or not, the administration would have to stop pretending as if student concerns didn't matter.

Meanwhile, my search for justice had gotten a lot more fruitful.

Carmody was in jail, awaiting trial. The list of charges was as long as my arm. Marcus had pressed charges for his assault after the school had asked him to cooperate with their case. Three of the boys who had attacked him had turned out to be underage and were now in juvenile detention. They banned the rest from campus, and they would face worse legal troubles. The campus was charging Carmody and his buddies for the arson and assorted acts of vandalism on top of the rest of the things they'd done.

Four others, the three freshmen who had tried to break down my door and the one who had come after me with scissors, were facing charges from the campus as well, and most of them were going down for the arson and assault too. The investigation was ongoing. I had already answered endless police questions. When they asked if I would testify, I told them I was looking forward to it.

I really was.

Courtroom drama was nothing compared to what I had already gone through, and I wouldn't have to face it alone.

But Carmody? He was about as alone in the world now as a guy could get.

Carmody's father had never contacted me, and I didn't expect him to. His mother hadn't either, aside from a fancy card sent to my dorm room with a short apology note. I didn't know if she sympathized with me, or if she had realized that her baby had doomed himself. I didn't care which. And I would not let a perfunctory apology impede my pressing charges, if that was her expectation. Very little about her, her husband's, or her son's actions made any sense to me at all.

She and her husband had spoiled, coddled, and protected that woman-hating monster when they should have been disciplining him and getting him into therapy. They had used their clout to let him make a nuisance of himself on campus and among the Alpha Omega. When he had tried to burn down a building, they had bailed him out within minutes of his being jailed. They had made their choices. They would have to deal with the consequences, along with their scumbag son. They deserved it.

Now, I could move on and think about things besides the danger caused by one asshole.

Things like friendship and being in love for the first time in my life.

I had told Billy about my five-on-one relationship a few weeks ago. It had been a practice run for telling Mom, and it had not been easy, but at least he hadn't judged me. He had stared at me openmouthed and asked if I had bitten off more than I could chew. He had asked for the complete story and gotten it, minus a lot of the sex and violence.

My Gentlemen were all the alpha-male type in different ways, and they were all determined to spoil me. He had laughed when I had said that. He had accused me of wrapping the most powerful guys on campus around my finger, no matter who they said ran the relationship. I had smiled.

Is it true? Maybe.

But my relationship with the Gentlemen was entirely mutual. And we were all putting the work in to keep everyone happy. And that was what was important.

They were talking about getting me an apartment again, some place large enough for more than one of them to stay over at a time. Even now, with no safety concerns, they seemed insistent. Maybe they didn't want the new batch of pledges teasing them about visiting a specific dorm room repeatedly. Maybe they wanted to spoil me even more. Whatever the reason, I didn't mind. It was their money. But I still had reservations about living in a space that I depended on others to pay for. But we would work it out somehow. Next to the craziness we had all faced together, that discussion seemed simple.

The fraternity house was slowly becoming like a second home. Some mornings, I woke up in one of their rooms instead of back here. I couldn't stay long—I could never be a member—but at least no one freaked out if they saw me coming down the stairs.

The men of Markinswell University had gotten used to my presence. Some, like the Gentlemen or my astrophysics classmates, were glad I was there. Others didn't care, and if anyone else had a problem with it, they were keeping quiet. When I told Mom the whole story, she would at least know that I was finally safe here. And she would know who to credit for that besides me.

Even if introducing all five of my boyfriends to her was still going to be a little awkward. No—a lot awkward. She was going to do much more than tease me when the time came. She would worry, like she always did. She would wonder how in the world such a complicated situation would work. And she would put every one of them to the test, to make sure they were worthy of her precious daughter.

I knew that, and I loved her for it, because I knew it all came from the heart. But I still wasn't looking forward to that conversation. I was new at love, and it would be a shock to her to learn that, unlike her sister, whom she thought of as so lucky, I had gotten very lucky early in the game.

Very lucky.

My phone pinged. Blake was downstairs. My smile came

back—not the professional one this time, but one bright and full of joy.

It was time to go see the men in my life again.

Grabbing my bag and my coat, I hurried out.

IF YOU LOVED HEARTBREAK KINGS, you're going to devour my enemies-to-lovers story featuring Core and Sin. Keep reading for a sneak peek at **TWISTED LIES!**

GET A FREE SEDONA VENEZ BOOK!

https://sedonavenez.com/free-book

Manhattan. Present Day. W.C. (With Core)

How the hell did this shit happen?

I fucking hate him, but I want him.

It was sick and sordid, and I couldn't tell what this really was. I only knew when I was around him, he suffocated me with his twisted lies and dirty secrets, only to cruelly resuscitate me. And shamefully, I loved it.

Core stepped forward, caging me alongside his desk, making sure my body was flush against his. "Ready to fuck, Sin?" he whispered in my ear.

I sucked in a breath as his hard bulge pressed into my stomach. Mesmerized, I watched his hand reach out. His callused fingers slid down my cheek before his thick thumb dragged across my bottom lip and penetrated the barrier of my wet, pouty lips. My body jerked at the sensual intrusion.

Honestly, I wasn't really sure how to process the touch of a man again. It'd been so long I'd forgotten just how good it felt to have a strong hand touching me.

He scowled. "Sin, don't move," he demanded huskily while grabbing the back of my head with his other hand. "Show me how much you want this, how much you want me. Lick it like you want it, darling."

I should stop him before this goes any further.

I knew I should, but my body thought otherwise. I was high off his lies and drunk off his hate. Now there was no way out. On cue, I ran my tongue along the length of his thumb as if it were his shaft. When he growled with pleasure, a tremor pulsed through my body as my cunt contracted.

Jesus, I'm so fucked.

Our mouths were a breath away. The desire and tension were almost more than I could take. Abruptly, he removed his thumb, still cupping the back of my neck, pulling hard on my hair, before his lips settled across my mouth. My breath caught, my mind undecided as to whether I should pull back or allow him to delve further.

Who am I kidding?

There was no allowing. I was Core's possession, and the cocky bastard knew it.

I moaned sensually as his tongue curled around mine, demanding it come out and play. He awakened a need that lay dormant in the pit of my stomach, a need only he could satisfy.

He skated his hand down and squeezed my hip while his eyes were fixed on mine. "I want you. Now," he growled.

My pulse raced, and my body trembled with want. He was crumbling my resolve. Diabolically, he stripped me bare emotionally, leaving me vulnerable and raw to the bone. He was revealing a piece of me that would be better left hidden. The message was clear. He knew what I needed, and he would give it to me if I took the leap of faith.

He smiled like the devil reincarnated as he released me and sat on the leather chair with his legs splayed. My stomach rolled with anxiousness as I leaped into the pits of scorching hell by pushing up the hem of my dress before straddling his legs. I shook my hair slowly as I rotated my hips. He grabbed my ass hard, stilling my movement.

I trailed my fingers over his chest. "Then take me, McKay, until there's nothing left." I leaned in toward him and bit his lower lip.

He gave me a bad-boy smile, causing my stomach to flip-flop like I was on a roller coaster.

"Sinful." He licked my bottom lip slowly. He pulled back with his eyes locked on to me with a power that left me breathless. "Are you mine?" he asked gruffly.

My heart raced with sickening excitement. I knew he was evil, lust, and darkness personified. He should have terrified me, but he didn't because I was just as fucked up in the head as he was.

"Always," I whispered.

"I'm never letting you go, Sin." Tilting my head back, he kissed me hard. "What I claim, I keep."

I was a spider trapped in his web.

"Now get on your knees," he ordered in a brusque tone.

This was it—the moment of truth that would seal my destiny. Self-preservation finally kicked in.

My mind screamed like a banshee, *Run, Sin! Tuck your ass and run!*

My body tightened, preparing to run away as if a horde of paparazzi was nipping at my stilettos.

Core's cold gray eyes narrowed. "I'm a hard-hearted, ruthless motherfucker who doesn't know shit about love or relationships." He pulled me forward, one hand taking a firm hold of my wrists, while his legs forced my knees apart. "And neither do you." His free hand ripped off my panties. "Perfection is complete fantasyland bullshit."

His hand slid against my pussy, and two fingers pushed inside, stretching me open. I moaned as I clenched around those fingers tightly.

"See, darling?" He smiled knowingly. "That's our reality. It's raw, wicked, and wild—a connection on a level very few will ever have or could even dream of."

I didn't have it all figured out. What I did know was Core was no Prince Charming, and I, for damn sure, wasn't a princess. There would be no fairy-tale ending for us. It would be hard work, and more importantly, it would be real. Life couldn't be all about tiaras and knights riding in to save the day.

Damn it! I would rewrite my fucking story and leap into the black abyss on faith alone because I wasn't looking for forever.

I licked his lips, unzipped his pants, and wrapped my hands around his hard cock before squeezing hard. He hissed as he relaxed against the soft leather chair, watching with intensity as I slid to my knees.

This was my give. This was his take.

And there was no going back.

Till death do us part...

Devour Core and Sin's story **TWISTED LIES!**

WANT FREE SEDONA VENEZ BOOKS?

Sign up for Sedona Venez's Newsletter and receive FREE BOOKS. In addition to the free stories, you will also get special pricing, exclusive previews and news of new releases.

GET A FREE SEDONA VENEZ BOOK!

Join Sedona's mailing list to be the first to know of new releases, free books, special prices and other author giveaways.

https://sedonavenez.com/free-book

ABOUT THE AUTHOR

USA TODAY BESTSELLING AUTHOR SEDONA VENEZ lives in New York City with her hot ex-military hubby —hooah—and their fur babies. She loves writing sizzling, sexy intricate stories about strong but broken characters who push limits, overcome their fears and risk it all for love.

Sedona loves to connect with readers!
www.sedonavenez.com